Two Maiden Aunts

Mary H. Debenham

THE TWO MAIDEN AUNTS.

Two Maiden Aunts

Mary H. Debenham

Illustrated by Gertrude D. Hammond

TWO MAIDEN AUNTS

BY

MARY H. DEBENHAM

AUTHOR OF 'MISTRESS PHIL' 'A LITTLE CANDLE ETC.

WITH ONE FULL-PAGE ILLUSTRATION
BY GERTRUDE D. HAMMOND

1895

BY THE SAME AUTHOR

THE MAVIS AND THE MERLIN. Price 2s.
MY GOD-DAUGHTER. Price 2s.
MOOR AND MOSS. Price 2s. 6d.
FOR KING AND HOME. Price 2s. 6d.
MISTRESS PHIL. Price 2s.
A LITTLE CANDLE. Price 3s. 6d.
FAIRMEADOWS FARM. Price 2s.
ST. HELEN'S WELL. Price 2s.

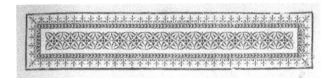

CONTENTS

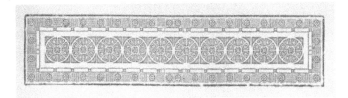

CHAPTER I

THE AUNTS

'Child, be mother to this child.' — E. B. BROWNING.

 t was seven o'clock on an autumn morning nearly a hundred years ago. A misty October morning, when the meadows looked grey with the heavy dew, and the sky was only just beginning to show pale blue through the haze which veiled it.

There was a certain little hamlet, just a few cottages clustered together beside a country road, where the world seemed hardly yet awake. The road ran across a wide common, where the cows and horses and geese wandered about pretty much as they chose, and the blackberries grew as they grow only on waste ground. The blackberry season was pretty nearly over, and the damp had taken the taste out of those which the village children had left, but the dewy nights were still warm enough to bring up the mushrooms like fairy tables in all directions, and there was at least one gatherer from the village who had been astir an hour ago, for the common was a well-known mushroom ground, and early birds had the best chance. He was coming back now with a goodly basketful, shaking showers of dew off the grass at every step and leaving a track of footmarks behind him. Through the mist he looked a sort of giant, but he was only a tall, sturdy lad of seventeen, in a fustian jacket and the wide hat which countrymen used to wear in the days of our grandfathers. He turned off the common before he reached the village and went down a little lane, at the end of which stood a small gabled house, in a garden where the autumn flowers hung their heads under the heavy dew. There was a paddock behind the house where a cow was feeding, and a gate led through a yard to the back door, and thither the boy was turning when he noticed a little girl in homespun frock and sun-bonnet leaning over the garden gate, looking up rather wistfully at the shuttered windows of the house. She gave a great start as the boy came behind her and laid his hand suddenly on her shoulder.

'Now then, Nance,' he said severely, 'what are you about, disturbing the place at this time in the morning?'

The little girl shook his hand off with an impatient shrug.

'What be you about, Pete, starting me like that? I'm not doing nothing nor disturbing nobody. I can look at the cottage, I suppose, without you to call me up for it?'

'Mother'll be fine and angry when she hears what you've been at,' said the boy, 'peeping and prying on the young ladies, and them in trouble.'

Nancy put up her pretty lip with the injured look of a spoilt child. 'I'm not peeping nor prying nor hurting nobody, and, if I am, what are you doing, I should like to know?' Then, as she noticed his basket, she clapped her hands with a little triumphant laugh.

'I know what 'tis you're after,' she cried; 'you've been off and got them mushrooms, and you've brought them for the young ladies so as you can see Penny or maybe Miss Betty herself, and hear whether it's really true. And haven't I got some eggs, my own hen's eggs, here for them, and only just waiting till they open the shutters to take them in?'

'Well, why don't you go round to the back door, as is the proper place for you,' said the stern elder brother, 'instead of staring at gentlefolks' houses like a great gawky?'

'Well, come to that, I know which is the biggest gawky of us two,' said pert little Nance; 'and, if you must know, I was just waiting for the chance of Miss Betty coming down, seeing Penny might be in one of her tantrums and not tell me a word.' Then, as the front door of the house suddenly opened, she exclaimed, joyously,

'Look, if she isn't there,' and was darting in at the gate, when her brother caught her and held her back. 'Come away, will you, ye interfering little hussy!' he was beginning hastily, when the girl who had opened the door caught sight of the two and came down the garden path towards them. Spoilt Nancy shook herself free, and with a triumphant glance at her big brother she ran to meet the young lady, and Peter could do nothing but follow her; and, indeed, if the truth must be told, he was not at all sorry to do it, and, perhaps, just a little grateful to naughty Nancy for showing the way.

The early riser from the cottage was a girl of thirteen, a very pretty little girl, with a fair, fresh face, sunshiny hazel eyes, and hair of that golden brown colour which the bracken wears in autumn. She seemed to have dressed in rather a hurry, for her long black frock was not quite perfectly fastened, the muslin scarf round her shoulders was just a little crooked, and the black ribbon which tied the bright hair had not managed to catch it all, so that a few curly locks came tumbling out at the side. She had shut the house door very quietly, and she held up her finger for a sign of silence as she came down the path; and Nancy, who had started off running to meet her, stopped as if a sudden feeling of shyness had come over her, a feeling, it must be owned, which didn't often trouble Nancy, certainly not towards Miss Betty Wyndham, whom she had known ever since she could remember. But then she had never seen Miss Betty look quite like this before, in her black frock and with such a grave look in her merry eyes, a look that was rather sad, and yet, perhaps, more serious than sad, and that somehow made Nancy stop and curtsey and Peter pull off his hat with that sort of shy respect which the most careless among us must pay to a fresh sorrow or loss. But, in spite of her grave look, Miss Betty seemed very pleased to see them.

'Good morning, Pete; good morning, Nancy,' she said. 'How kind of you to come so early! Did you guess I should be down?'

'I thought maybe you would, miss,' said Nancy, 'only the shutters being up I thought you must be asleep still.'

'I dressed in the dark,' said Miss Betty, giving her scarf a little tug which didn't straighten it much, 'because I didn't want to wake Angel. Poor Angel, she was so late coming to bed last night; I'd been asleep ever so long and woken up again while she was talking to Penny.'

And then she stopped and looked from one to the other with a questioning look in her eyes.

'You know, don't you?' she said at last; 'you've heard about the sad thing that's happened?'

For once in a way Nancy left her brother to answer.

'We haven't heard nothing for certain, Miss Betty,' he said, 'only people talked, and we knew Penny had gone to fetch you home; but father said we weren't to say nothing till we knew for certain.'

'It's quite true,' said Miss Betty gravely,' quite dreadfully true, Pete. Our brother, Mr. Bernard, has been killed in the West Indies, and we are very poor now; we have left school and come home to live.'

I fear that the last piece of news so much did away with the sadness of the first that Nancy's face broadened into a delighted smile, and she only just cut short an exclamation of joy. Luckily Miss Betty was not looking at her, and she saw Peter's frown and felt a little ashamed of herself.

'I want to tell you everything,' Miss Betty went on; 'it was very nice of your father not to want people to talk, but now we should like every one to know because we are very proud of my brother, and we want our friends to be. Will you come into the arbour and I'll tell you?' and she led the way across the garden while Peter and Nancy followed willingly enough. The arbour was that sort of bower which we see in old-fashioned pictures and sing about in old songs. There

4

had been roses climbing over it all the summer, and a few blossoms hung there still, pale and fragrant, among a tangle of clematis and everlasting peas. On the little grass plot just outside the arbour there was a stone figure, not like the nymphs and Cupids and water-carriers which we find in trim old-fashioned gardens and stately pleasure grounds, but the chipped worn figure of a lady, lying with folded hands and a quaint head-dress and straight falling hair. No one quite knew where that statue came from, except that it must have lain once upon a tomb in some church or monastery chapel, and in evil days, when men had forgotten their reverence for holy ground and the quiet dead, the tomb must have been destroyed, and the figure defaced and thrown out as rubbish. Then some one later on had brought her to the cottage and set her up as an ornament to the garden, leaning against a tree, and looking very strange and uncomfortable. When Betty and her sister were little children they were half afraid of the tall grim figure, which looked queer and uncanny among the bushes in the twilight, but as they grew older and knew more about her, they lost their fear of her and began to be sorry for her, and they got Peter and some of the village boys to move her out of her unnatural position and lay her down on the grass as she had once lain on her tomb in the church, and planted flowers beside her. And the great purple convolvulus, or, as I love to call it by its sweet old name, the Morning Glory, seeded itself every year, and twined its soft tendrils and opened its lovely flowers all about the poor lady, as if it wanted to hide all the marks of hard usage, and the grass made her a soft pillow, and the pink rose petals dropped all about her, and she looked as if she were happily asleep among the flowers. And when she was being moved the boys came upon some other pieces of stone among the bushes, which might have been part of the same tomb. There was one bit with part of a coat-of-arms on it which no one could make out, and another bit with some letters, many of them quite defaced, but after a lot of puzzling and rubbing the moss off, the little girls managed to read the two words, 'Demoiselle Jehanne.' Miss Angelica felt sure it was French, and she copied it out and took it back to school to ask her schoolmistress what it meant. And the mistress said she was right, it was most likely old Norman-French such as was talked in England five or six hundred years ago, and that 'demoiselle' was the title of a young lady, and 'Jehanne' was the old way of writing Jeanne or Jane. So Angelica and Betty decided directly that it must be the name of their stone lady, and called her 'Demoiselle Jehanne,' or, to make it clearer to Peter and their other village friends, 'Miss Jane.' And it was wonderful what a companion Miss Jane had become to them: they never felt really alone when they were sitting beside her. Betty made up stories about her, and Angelica wondered about her and about the days when she was alive, and how old she was when she died, and whether she ever saw Edward the Black Prince, and whether she had a father and a mother who were very sad when they put that figure over her grave. And often when anything had gone wrong with the sisters, they would come and sit down on the grass by the arbour and tell it to Miss Jane, and feel as if she sympathized with them and comforted them. And if more lucky little girls are inclined to laugh at them, I would ask them to be thankful that they are happier than my two little sisters, and have a mother to whom they can go and tell their troubles instead of whispering them into the broken stone ear of Miss Jane.

And perhaps it was partly that old custom of theirs that made Betty at this moment, when she wanted to tell about the great change that was coming into her life, lead the way to the arbour and sit down on the bench close to the silent figure among the trailing creepers. Peter and Nancy stood in front of her and waited for her to speak, both a little embarrassed, as we are when we aren't quite sure how we ought to feel and what we ought to say. It was very sad, of course, about Mr. Bernard Wyndham being dead, but, as they had neither of them ever seen him in their lives, it was rather difficult to mind very much. But then they knew they ought to think about what Miss Betty was feeling. Nancy looked at Pete and felt that it would be dreadful to have one's brother killed, even if he did scold one and keep one in order rather too much. But then a brother who had been in the West Indies for twelve out of the thirteen years of one's life was different from a brother who was always there to get one blackberries and lift one over hedges, and even box one's ears when one required it. And besides, as I have said, Miss Betty did not look exactly very sad, only grave and just the least little bit important. So they waited to hear what she had to say.

'It is quite true, Pete and Nancy,' she began; 'Mr. Bernard has been killed in a dreadful rising of the natives in the West Indian Islands. He was very, very brave—of course we knew he would be that—and he has died as an Englishman ought to die, so we shall never be able to show him all the things we wanted to show him, and to introduce him to all of you here, as we always thought we should.' Miss Betty's voice began to shake a little for the first time, and Pete and Nancy waited in respectful silence. After a minute she went on:

'But Angel says we must try to be very proud to think of him dying so bravely, for she says that women all over England are giving up so much, that we ought to be glad to think that we have given something too. And now I am coming to the part that is the most surprising. Only think—our brother was married, married out there eight years ago, and he never told us! I suppose he wanted to give us a beautiful surprise when he brought us a new sister home.'

She waited for somebody to say something. Peter's face did not look as if he thought the surprise a very beautiful one.

'Beg your pardon, Miss Betty,' he said doubtfully, 'but Mr. Bernard's lady, she'd—she'd be black, I suppose?'

'Black!' exclaimed Betty in horror. 'Oh, dear me, no, Peter! Of course she wouldn't be black. There are English people in the West Indies or my brother wouldn't have been there, and it was an English lady he married; but, poor lady, she died when she'd only been our sister not quite a year. I suppose that was why Bernard never told us afterwards, because of not wanting us to know what we'd missed. It was very, very brave and very unselfish of him, of course, but Angel and I wish he had, because then we could have written and said how sorry we were, and perhaps comforted him a little. And now I'm coming to the most surprising thing of all. My brother had a little boy, and he is seven years old now, and he is in England and he will be here to-night.' Miss Betty hurried out these last pieces of news one on the top of the other, and then stopped and looked at her hearers, who certainly seemed surprised enough to satisfy her.

'Poor little gentleman!' said kind-hearted Peter, ''tis a sad coming to England for him, for sure, and him an orphan and alone in the world, as one may say.'

'No, Peter, one mayn't say anything of the kind,' said Miss Betty, pulling herself up and looking as dignified as she possibly could. 'Of course, he's an orphan, poor dear little boy! but he can't be alone in the world at all when he's got two aunts, and his aunt Angelica and I will take good care he never feels like an orphan, the darling.'

Nancy's eyes opened their very widest. 'But, Miss Betty,' she said, 'I thought aunts were old people.'

'Oh, Nancy!' said Betty, with an air of wisdom; 'you have a very great deal to learn, Nancy, dear. It is not the age that makes the aunt, Nancy, it is the nephew or the niece. And as for being old, Angelica and I aren't so very young. She was sixteen last winter and I am thirteen, and people have done a great deal at thirteen, as you'll learn when you read biography. And, even if we haven't been so very old before, we have to begin now and grow up at once, for we are going to live here and be independent ladies, with our cousin, Mr. Crayshaw, coming down now and then from London to see us, and—and talk over business, and advise us about our money matters, and we shall have Godfrey, our nephew Godfrey, to take care of and educate. Angel says,' she went on after a minute, while the faces of her listeners showed great satisfaction at the arrangements, 'that we must put everything else on one side and bring up our nephew as his father would have wished, to be a proper English gentleman and a credit to his family. She says we can fit ourselves to do any duty that we have got to do, and our duty now is to be good aunts, and we must be *that* with all our might;' and here the good aunt broke off suddenly as her eye fell for the first time on the baskets which her listeners were holding.

'Did you bring those for us?' she exclaimed. 'Oh, how kind of you! Are those Polly's eggs, Nance? I guessed they were, and the mushrooms are off the common, I know. Whereabouts did you get them, Pete? I must go with you some day very soon, I'm longing——'

And then as if with a sudden recollection the eager little lady pulled herself up, smoothed her crooked kerchief, and shook the rebellious hair out of her eyes, and went on in her most sober tones: 'I don't know, Peter, whether I shall be able to come mushrooming much now. Of course my nephew will take up a good deal of my time, and I'm not sure whether many mushrooms are quite a good thing for children. But eggs will be very nice for his breakfast—a new-laid egg every day, I think, not too hard-boiled. And there's just one more little thing; I hope you won't mind, but I fancy if you could get into the way of calling us Miss Angelica and Miss Elizabeth when our nephew is there it would be a good thing, and make him look up to us more. You won't mind my saying so, will you? And now I think I must go, because Angel—because Miss Angelica will be up; so good-bye, and thank you very much indeed for coming.'

And the next minute Miss Betty was gone, starting off in her usual whirlwind fashion, then pulling herself up and marching along solemnly and with the dignity which became the aunt.

But she forgot her dignity when she got upstairs, and met her sister coming out of her bedroom to look for her with a little shade of anxiety in her face. Angelica Wyndham was one of those very gentle, thoughtful people who are so tender about their neighbours' happiness, so fearful of hurting and slow to put their own wishes forward, that we hardly know how powerful that very gentleness makes them in their little world. Everybody loved Angel, and said how sweet she was and how pretty; but they hardly knew how they came to consider her and to go out of their way to please her, just because she always thought so much about other people that really it was a shame to vex her. She was not particularly quick, except with that sort of quickness which we can all learn by being thoughtful for others, and watchful to please and help them. She was not nearly so clever as Betty, and she knew it quite well, and was never a bit jealous when Betty passed her in class and learnt her lessons in half the time; and Betty, on her side, thought there was no one in all the world like Angel and would have done anything to please her, and always hoped that one day she might be half as wise and good. And so this morning, when she saw her sister standing in the doorway, with the little worried anxious look in her gentle eyes, she flung her arms round her, and stood on tip-toe to kiss her, exclaiming eagerly:

'Angel dear, did you wonder where I was? Did I wake you getting up? I left the blinds down on purpose. I've only been talking to Pete and Nancy, and telling them all about it, and Nancy's brought us some eggs, and Pete's got such a basket of mushrooms!'

'You haven't been on the common for mushrooms this morning, have you, dear?' asked Angelica.

'Oh no, no, of course not, Angel; how could I? No, I told him perhaps I shouldn't be able to go with him now. You needn't be afraid, Angel, I've told him all about it, and how we are going to grow up now at once, as we have to be Godfrey's maiden aunts; and I told him to call me Miss Elizabeth, and he quite understands.'

Angel, with an arm round Betty's neck among the tumbled curls, wondered, in her gentle way, whether her eager young sister quite understood herself, but all she said was:

'Come in and let me tie your hair, Betty dear.'

'Isn't it tidy?' said Betty, with a pull at her loose locks; then, as she stopped beside the looking-glass, and caught sight of herself in contrast to Angelica's graceful figure, looking taller and slimmer in the straight black dress, with the soft muslin about her slender throat and the dark abundant curls falling smoothly on her shoulders, she exclaimed in dismay,

'Oh, Angel dear, I'm so sorry! I dressed in the dark.'

'I know, Betty dear. Sit down and let me do your hair,' said the elder sister, getting the ribbon off with as little pulling of the tangled curls as possible.

'You see,' she said very gently and diffidently, as she set to work to put Betty in order, 'I've been thinking a great deal about this dear little boy of ours, and, Betty, it makes me feel so young.'

'Does it?' said Betty, twisting her head round so as to look into her sister's face; 'why, Angel dear, it makes me feel old!'

'Yes, I know what you mean. I mean it makes me feel silly and inexperienced when I ought to be wise. You see, Betty, I think we ought both to consider that we haven't got Bernard's little boy to please ourselves with him, and pet him, and give him everything he wants. He won't be a plaything for us—we have to make a man of him, and as he hasn't any one else to look to, we mustn't let him just take us for playfellows, he must look upon us as——'

'As his maiden aunts,' said Betty, emphatically; 'yes, Angel, I quite see that.'

'You see,' Angelica went on, 'I expect when we get the dear little thing to ourselves we shall find it much easier to romp with him and pet him and all that, and so we might if there were any one else older and wiser for him to look up to; but it wouldn't do for a little boy only to have playfellows, there must be some one for him to respect.'

'And as there isn't any one else, it must be us,' said Betty, decidedly, 'for he won't have any one else belonging to him to respect except Cousin Crayshaw about once a fortnight, which isn't very often, and so we shall have to be instead of a father and mother and uncles and aunts and grandmothers and everybody that little boys have to respect all rolled into one.'

'And not think at all about pleasing ourselves with him as if he were a kitten,' said Angel, gravely; 'you see things so quickly, Betty dear——'

But there her sentence was cut short by Betty springing up suddenly and flinging both arms round her.

'Angel,' she cried, 'if you talk like that I'll never forgive you. If he can't be good with you to teach him he doesn't deserve to have you for his relation. And you are always to scold me—only it mustn't be when he is there—if I forget about growing up and do stupid things and make myself so that he can't respect me. And perhaps by-and-bye, if you tell me, and I try very hard indeed, I may get to be a real, good, proper, sensible maiden aunt.'

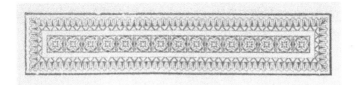

CHAPTER II

THE NEPHEW

'Hers is a spirit deep and crystal clear:
Calmly beneath her earnest face it lies,
Free without boldness, meek without a fear,
Quicker to look than speak its sympathies.'—LOWELL.

s Betty Wyndham had said, she and Angel were not very well off for relations. Angelica's memory held some faint, faraway pictures of mother and father, which she had dreamt over so often that they were always fair and tender like the hazy distance of an autumn landscape. Dimly, too, she could recollect the time of loss and loneliness and half-understood grief when she cried herself to sleep at night for want of the familiar kisses, and she had hazy remembrances of strange faces and changes, and a time when the cottage by Oakfield Common was a new home, and Cousin Amelia Crayshaw, the elderly relation, with whom she and Betty were to live (and who had died two years before this story begins), was a stranger—a rather alarming stranger, so unlike mamma, that it seemed unnatural to go to her for things, and ask her questions, and say the Catechism to her on Sunday.

And there was one other recollection which Angel had thought of and talked to Betty about so often, that it made quite a landmark in her life: the recollection of a day in that dreary time when she sat, a little lonely, frightened child, only dimly understanding the meaning of her black frock, by the cradle where baby Betty was asleep, crying in a hushed, awed way, as much at the grave faces and the drawn blinds as because papa and mamma had gone away, for they must surely come back by-and-bye.

Then her nurse Penelope looked into the darkened room, with a face swollen with crying, and said in a whisper, 'Miss Angel dear, speak to your brother,' and pushed in a lad whom Angel had never seen before, and went away, treading softly as every one did in the shadowed house. Little Angel left off crying and looked up at the stranger, who stood there by the door, with a white set face of pain which frightened her. Then she got up obediently and came to him, and held up a little pale face to be kissed, as she had learnt to do to her friends. And the tall lad caught her up suddenly and held her tight in a clasp which hurt her, and sat down in her little chair and burst into strong weeping over her curly hair. And Angel, frightened as she was, knew she ought to try and comfort him, and so stroked the hands that held her so tightly, and whispered tremulously that by-and-bye papa and mamma would be coming back, for Penny had cried over her because they were gone away, and this mysterious brother must be grieving about it too. And once or twice he said out loud, 'I did love them! I did love them!' and his voice sounded quite fierce, only he held her so close all the time that Angel felt he could not be angry with her. And then baby Betty woke and cried, and the four-year-old sister and the big brother soothed her between them, until Penny came back to the door and called softly, and cried afresh to see the young gentleman with Betty in his arms and Angel holding on to his coat. And he kissed them both quickly and went away, and Angelica never saw him again. He went abroad, she knew, very soon afterwards, for Penny told her to pray that the ship might not go down on the way; but Cousin Amelia never talked about him, and Angel, with the quick intuition of a little child, soon learnt that she did not care to speak of him. But if Angel spoke little she thought the more.

All her pitiful little heart had gone out to the big brother who had cried so about papa and mamma, and had said he loved them as Angel loved them herself, and had hushed Betty to sleep, and held her and kissed her as kind, quiet Cousin Amelia never did.

When she and Betty grew older and went to school, and heard other girls talk about their brothers, Angel added all the good things she learnt to her fancies about her brother abroad, and Betty's active imagination improved upon the picture, until they hardly knew how much of it was their own painting and how much belonged to that dim recollection of Angel's childhood.

And now the fancies had come suddenly to an end which was real enough, and the brother would never come home to live with them and play with them, and let them mend his clothes and knit his stockings as other sisters did. And, instead, they had to get used to the strange idea of the dead unknown wife, and the little son for whose sake they were to grow up into wise sober women before they had done with being little girls. What wonder that Angel looked pale and grave after a wakeful night, and that Betty felt that madcap ways and tumbled curls must cease from this day forward.

Little Nancy Rogers, hurrying home so as to get there before Peter, felt herself a person of importance, with such news to tell. Her father was gardener at Oakfield Place, the most important building in the village, an ivied house with a garden full of sweet, old-fashioned flowers, planted by the late mistress who had died six years before. The present owner, Captain Maitland, was a naval officer, away with his ship, and the house was empty except for the Rogers family, who lived in some of the back rooms that Mrs. Rogers might keep the place in order. Before she married she had been maid to Miss Amelia Crayshaw, and still came in now and then when Penny wanted extra help; and her children and the two little ladies had been playfellows, for Angel and Betty had no girl friends near their home, and, when Cousin Amelia would let them, were happy enough to spend their holidays running about the old garden with the little Rogers, getting mushrooms and blackberries under Peter's charge, or, on wet days, playing 'hide and seek' about the empty house. And even Cousin Amelia, who was very particular about their manners and the company they kept, admitted that Martha Rogers' children could not teach them any harm. Indeed, it was Betty who now and then led the whole party into scrapes, for which, however, she was always ready enough to bear the blame.

So that there was no house in Oakfield where the news of Mr. Bernard's death and the arrival of his little son was received with more interest than at the Rogers', even though Nancy did get a scolding for going off to the cottage and taking up Miss Betty's time without a word to any one at home. But Nancy was the baby and a little spoilt even by her sensible mother, and it took a good deal of scolding to put her out of conceit with herself; so, though she had strict orders on no account to go to the cottage again till she was sent for, she managed to be by the roadside at that hour in the evening when Mr. Crayshaw's post-chaise always arrived on the occasions of his visits to Oakfield. And so she saw the chaise and the horses, and a black box on the top, but it was too dark for even her inquisitive black eyes to get a peep at the travellers. And in the twilight of the October evening the two young aunts were awaiting the nephew who was to be henceforward such a great part of their lives. Angel stood in the cottage porch under a tangle of twining creepers, looking gravely out into the shadows. It seemed to her as if, out of that darkness, something strange and great were coming to her— new duties, new cares and thoughts, which would change her from a quiet, obedient little girl into a wise, thoughtful woman. And, with very little confidence in her own power or wisdom, she was trying to be brave and making up her mind to do her best. Betty's clear voice on the stairs roused her from her grave thoughts.

'No, not meat to-night, Penny, it's too late; it isn't good for children to have heavy suppers; only the bread-and-milk, please, and do, do take care not to burn the milk, because I know quite well how horrid it was when they burnt it at school.'

'Bless your heart, Miss Betty dear,' was the answer, 'one'd think I never made a basin of bread-and-milk in my life instead of feeding you as a baby and Miss Angel before you.'

But if Betty heard the remark she did not wait to answer it, for she was in the porch by her sister's side before Penelope had finished.

'Angel, can you hear wheels? I fancy I do; I think they'll be here in a minute, don't you? I hope I shall remember all the things I wanted to say. Aren't you excited, Angel? Only I suppose maiden aunts oughtn't ever to be very excited. Let's try to be calm. I don't feel very calm, do you?'

'Not very,' Angel said. Her colour was coming and going, and the arm that she put round Betty trembled, but she stood quite still. Old Penelope came to the door behind them and asked almost as anxiously as Betty if they heard anything, and said something a little doubtfully about it being a damp evening for standing there in the porch, but she did not call them to come in, only stood there and strained eyes and ears in the dim light. After all Angelica heard the wheels first and gave a start as they broke the silence, and there was time after that for Betty to rush indoors and poke up the fire before the chaise stopped at the garden gate. And then it was Betty who reached the gate first, with Penelope just behind her, for Angel was so unused to coming to the front that somehow she let them both pass her. And so Betty had hold of the door-handle first, and was trying to see through the steamy window almost before the horses stopped.

'There he is, the darling!' she exclaimed; 'I see him. Godfrey dear, I'm your aunt Elizabeth; come and let me kiss you.'

'Bless him for his papa's own boy,' puffed Penny behind her. 'I knew your dear papa, love.'

And at this moment the door opened suddenly, and the two received into their arms a thin, severe-looking gentleman, with scanty grey hair and a rather annoyed expression of face.

'Good gracious, Elizabeth, what is the meaning of this?' he exclaimed, as Betty clasped him round the waist in the dark. 'Penelope, what in the world are you doing? Is the whole place gone demented?'

Penny fell back in great confusion, but Betty was undaunted.

'I beg your pardon, Cousin Crayshaw,' she said, 'it wasn't you I meant to kiss—I thought you were Godfrey. Isn't Godfrey here?'

'Your brother's child is here of course,' said Mr. Crayshaw rather sharply, and turning back to the carriage, he said:

'Godfrey, come here and get out at once; don't keep every one waiting.'

'I won't!' said a very decided voice from the darkness inside the big chaise.

'You will do as you are told,' said Mr. Crayshaw severely; 'come out at once.'

'I won't!' said the voice again.

'Perhaps he's frightened,' suggested Betty, peeping in under her cousin's arm. 'Godfrey dear, I'm your Aunt Elizabeth. Come and have your supper, dear, I am sure you're hungry.'

'I don't want my Aunt Elizabeth, nor my supper,' said the rebellious voice from the chaise. 'I am going to turn this carriage the other way, and the horses will take me to the ship, and the ship will take me home.'

'The horses will take you to the stable, sir,' said the exasperated Mr. Crayshaw, 'and you can stay there if you prefer it to obeying me.'

'They will take me to the ship,' said the child's voice inside.

'They will do nothing of the kind, because you are to come with me instantly,' said the gentleman, with his foot on the step.

He made a dive into the chaise, there was the sound of a scuffle, then the clear voice could be heard exclaiming:

'Bad man, you are to let me go.'

'I shall do nothing of the sort, sir.'

'Then I'll be a leech.'

The next moment there was a sort of spring from a little dark figure, and Mr. Crayshaw stumbled out of the chaise, with a small boy holding tightly to his leg.

'Let go of me directly, you abominable child!' he cried, but the small arms only tightened their grip of his knee, the thin legs twisted closely round his ankle, and I am afraid even that a set of very white sharp little teeth were fastened in the black knee breeches. Poor Mr. Crayshaw! It was not a dignified position for a very stiff and solemn London lawyer to have to hop along a gravelled path with a little boy hanging on to his leg. He made a desperate attempt to unclasp the clutching fingers, but the sharp teeth were so uncomfortably near his hand that he gave that up and tried kicking. It did not make it easier for him either to know that his appearance had been quite too much for the auntly gravity of Betty, who had her hands over her face to keep herself from screaming with laughter, while the driver and the postilion were watching with their mouths expanded into broad grins.

How it would have ended I cannot say; but at this moment Angelica came forward, standing just in the broad ray of light that streamed through the open door. She had put on a white dress, with a broad black sash, and her tall white figure caught Godfrey's eye. He still held on tightly to Mr. Crayshaw, but he called to her, in a voice half trembling, half defiant:

'I'm not afraid of you.'

'I don't want you to be, Godfrey,' said Angel, dreadfully puzzled as to what she ought to do.

'I'm a bad boy,' announced her nephew, with a fresh grip of his victim's leg, 'but if you turn me into a scorpion I'll sting him and kill him.'

Betty tried to stifle a fresh explosion of laughter; Angel looked in dismay at Mr. Crayshaw's black face, then stooped down and laid her gentle hand quickly on Godfrey's arm.

'Let go, dear, there's a good boy,' she said softly. 'Please do, because I want to speak to you.'

Her nephew looked straight at her for a moment, and then suddenly relaxed his hold and dropped down on the path at her feet. Mr. Crayshaw, feeling, perhaps, that he would gain nothing by stopping to scold, and just a little afraid of being seized by the other leg, muttered something indistinctly and walked into the house, limping a little, for Godfrey's feet and fingers had left their mark. Angel stooped down and laid her hand on the little boy's shoulder, and he caught hold of her dress and looked up in her face.

'I know all about you,' he said; 'you're a white witch. I am a bad boy, but I'm going to be good now, quite good. If I do everything you tell me, and promise not to be a leech again, and give you all the money in my pocket, will you make me into a bird, so that I can fly over the sea and back home to Biddy? Will you, white witch, will you?'

He had risen to his feet and was looking at her with such a white earnest face, and she could feel the thin little hands trembling as they clutched her dress. Angelica hardly knew what to say with those great eyes, grey eyes like Betty's, devouring her face.

'Godfrey, dear,' she said gently, 'you're mistaken, dear, I'm not a witch at all; I'm your papa's sister. I loved your papa and I want to love you, if you'll let me. I want you to come into the house with me, and I know you will be good.'

The child looked steadily at her for a minute, as if to make quite sure that she was speaking the truth, then his lips suddenly began to quiver.

'Can't I—can't I—go back, then?' he said, pressing his thin little hands tight together.

'We want you to try and be happy here with us,' said Angel very gently.

The bitter disappointment that swept over the little white face went to her heart. She put her arm tenderly round the boy, and felt that he was quivering all over from head to foot; he had set his teeth hard and was clasping his hands tightly, as if to force the tears back. He looked such a small, fragile thing with the black lines of weariness under his big, sad eyes; the only wonder was that he had managed to give poor Mr. Crayshaw so much trouble. Now when Angelica put her arm around him, his courage seemed to give way all at once, he gave a sort of gasp, and his voice ran up into a shrill little quaver.

'Take me where he can't see,' he faltered, and Angel, without another word, bore him off into the house and upstairs with his face hidden against her.

I think we must admit that poor Mr. Crayshaw had had a good deal to try him that evening. He had come down from London after some very disagreeable business there, and, as we can imagine, the journey had not been a very pleasant one. Then there had been that dreadful arrival, when Betty and the driver and the postilion had all laughed at him. And now, here at Oakfield Cottage, where his wishes were always treated with the greatest respect, he was kept waiting full twenty minutes for his supper. He rang the bell twice without getting any answer, but a third tremendous tug brought Penelope down, rather breathless and excited.

'Beg your pardon, sir, did you ring, sir?'

'I rang three times,' said Mr. Crayshaw severely, 'to ask whether the young ladies think of supping this evening.'

'I am sure I humbly beg pardon, sir,' said Penelope, who was dreadfully afraid of Mr. Crayshaw; 'the young ladies were just taken up with the poor dear little gentleman, bless him.'

'Hum!' said Mr. Crayshaw, with a dry little cough; 'still as the fact of the young gentleman being in the house does not prevent my wishing for something to eat, I should be glad if you would bring supper in any moment of time you can spare from his company.'

'Oh, I'm sure, sir, directly, sir,' stammered Penny, hurrying out of the room, and the next minute her voice might have been heard in very loud whispers to Angelica on the stairs, before she bustled down in double quick time to the kitchen. A minute or two later Betty came in with an air of much importance.

'Cousin Crayshaw, Angel and I beg your pardon for keeping you waiting for supper,' she said; 'we were putting Godfrey to bed. He seemed so strange, and so frightened, poor darling!'

'Humph!' coughed Mr. Crayshaw again, 'his behaviour has not given me that impression so far. I warn both you and Angelica that if you persist in making a martyr of an exceedingly spoilt and ill-disposed child, my only alternative will be to send him at once to some strict school where he will be properly dealt with.'

The colour rushed into Betty's cheeks and her lips opened for a hasty reply, when Angel came quickly into the room with a tray in her hands. Betty ran to help her while she made her gentle apology for being late. Penny had been upstairs with them, but they would help her now, and supper would be ready in a minute. She feared Cousin Crayshaw must be very hungry and cold too, perhaps; she hoped he was not fatigued by the journey from London. It was almost impossible to be angry with Angel, and Mr. Crayshaw relented a little, and said no more about Godfrey; indeed, remembering how Betty had laughed at his predicament, he was perhaps not very anxious to talk about the arrival. It was a very silent supper. Betty kept beginning to talk and pulling herself up, and Angel devoted herself to attending to Mr. Crayshaw, trying to keep him from missing Penelope, who usually waited on them, but who had stolen upstairs as soon as supper was served.

She came back when the meal was over to clear away, and behind the gentleman's back made signs to Angel that Godfrey was asleep; and Angel gently stopped Betty, who seemed inclined to slip out of the room, and took her own worsted work to a chair by the hearth opposite her cousin. Mr. Crayshaw had a newspaper, but he sat looking over it at the burning logs with a decidedly annoyed expression, and when the table was cleared and Penelope gone, he laid it down and turned to his two young cousins.

'How old are you, Angelica?' he asked abruptly.

'Nearly seventeen, Cousin Crayshaw,' answered the girl, 'and Betty is thirteen.'

'But I feel a great deal more than thirteen, Cousin Crayshaw,' said Betty, leaning over the back of Angelica's chair.

'I am glad to hear it,' said Mr. Crayshaw rather drily; 'I trust at any rate that you will be able to show some of the discretion which your peculiar circumstances will require.'

He cleared his throat and began again, while Angel laid down her work respectfully:

'You are possibly aware that the sudden death of your father, followed a few days later by that of your mother, left their affairs in much confusion. The greater part of their fortune went by law to your elder brother, a moderate sum being devoted to the expenses of your education. I regret that the investment of the small property accruing to yourselves has been less successful than could have been wished. As you probably know, the conduct of your brother has been from first to last unsatisfactory—most unsatisfactory.'

Betty glanced up sharply. Angel said gently,

'I know he loved my papa and mamma.'

'He showed his affection in an extraordinary manner,' said Mr. Crayshaw grimly; 'he was idle and extravagant in his early youth, and his career since then has been far from brilliant, not to speak of this most unfortunate and imprudent marriage with a penniless orphan girl, which he had sufficient shame to keep secret from his relations and advisers in England. When I heard of his death I naturally looked upon you and your sisters as heirs to the small property which I have managed to the best of my ability, and which would make a comfortable provision for you. And now it appears that this child, who was at first believed to have perished at the same time, has by some extraordinary chance survived, and of course inherits everything. A most unfortunate occurrence altogether.'

I think Mr. Crayshaw in his vexation had almost forgotten that he was not talking to himself, but he was suddenly reminded, for at this moment Angel stood up, looking very pale, but with a strange light burning in her eyes.

'Cousin Crayshaw,' she said, and there was a new ring in her quiet tones, 'you said a minute ago that it is time Betty and I were growing up. I think you must have forgotten that, and must think us either very childish or very heartless, or you would not speak as you have just done before us. Godfrey's father was our brother and he is dead, and whatever he has done that is wrong, I think no friend of ours should speak of it before us. And if you really mean that it is a misfortune for us that our brother's little boy is not dead, I hope you will never say such a thing again to us, or to any one. If his mother had lived we should have loved her dearly, and welcomed her for our sister, and now that we have only him left it will be the most sacred work of our lives to care for him, and teach him, and work for him too if he is poor.'

Angelica had never made such a speech in her life, certainly she had never dreamt of making it to Mr. Crayshaw, whom she had always looked upon with the greatest respect as a grown-up man, and her guardian. Betty felt as if she hardly knew her sister, but never in her life had she felt so proud of her. She stood up by Angel's side and put her arm through hers, and faced Mr. Crayshaw as if she were longing to fight Godfrey's battles directly.

'I won't touch one penny of his money,' she said, with her hair thrown back and her cheeks glowing, 'and I'd scrub and sweep for him gladly, that I would.'

Mr. Crayshaw got up and gave his chair an impatient push back.

'Don't let us have heroics, Elizabeth,' he said sharply. Then he glanced at Angel, walked over to the window and came back again.

'Angelica,' he began, 'I'—and there he hesitated. It was on the tip of his tongue to say, 'I am sorry I said what I did; I beg your pardon.' What a pity it was he didn't go on! If he had, Angel and Betty would have respected him more than they ever did before; but then we are apt to forget that people would really think more of us if they knew we were not ashamed to own ourselves in the wrong. But he did not finish his sentence, he went on after a minute:

'All I mean you to understand is the necessity for economy for you all if this child is to be put to school and started in life. I have considered the desirability of a lady companion for you, but no one presents herself to me at present, and I see no alternative but for the child to remain here with you until he is old enough for school. I shall spend every alternate Sunday here, and Penelope will do all that is necessary. You, Angelica, are of an age when young ladies should know something of housekeeping. As for the boy, he appears to have been thoroughly spoilt and mismanaged, and I can only say that if I find that you indulge him in such exhibitions as—as we have already seen, I must make other arrangements. You understand me?'

'Yes, Cousin Crayshaw,' said Angel quietly.

She sat down again, and took up her wool-work, but her fingers trembled so that the needle missed the proper holes. Betty dropped down on to a stool at her feet, and they sat in silence while Mr.

Crayshaw took the lamp to a side table and began to write. Presently Betty stole upstairs, and at nine o'clock Angel too rose, went over to her cousin, and held out her hand.

'Good night, Cousin Crayshaw,' she said.

Her cousin gave a look at her as she stood in the lamplight in her white dress and black ribbons. She was pale still, and he could see she had been crying, and felt sorry that he had hurt her. He had always thought of her as a little schoolgirl, but this evening it seemed as if she were growing into a woman. He took her hand, and held it a little longer than usual.

'Good night, Angelica,' he said, and then he cleared his throat and added:

'I feel sure that you will be a good girl, a—a sensible girl.'

'I will try to,' Angel said gently, and she went upstairs.

Betty was in the little room opening out of their own which the sisters had chosen for Godfrey. She was kneeling by the little boy's bed, looking at him, and almost holding her breath lest she should wake him.

'Fast asleep, dear little darling!' she whispered. 'Oh, Angel, how could he? Wicked man! Fancy if he hadn't us to protect him.'

'Hush,' whispered Angelica gravely, 'hush; you mustn't, Betty.'

She stooped down and dropped a light kiss on Godfrey's hair, and then drew her sister away from the bed to the window. The mists had cleared away, there was going to be a frost, and overhead the stars were bright.

Angel leaned against the window-frame and looked out with very serious eyes. 'Betty,' she said softly, 'we must never say a word about—about what happened downstairs this evening to any one, not even to each other, and we mustn't think about it, or we shall fancy things. Cousin Crayshaw is our guardian, and he wants to be our good friend. And he is right in saying that we must be very wise and very careful. And we must be fair, Betty, quite fair to him and Godfrey both, and teach Godfrey to respect him because it is his duty, and not excuse him when he is naughty like he was to-night. You will do that, won't you, dear?'

'If you'll help me, Angel,' said Betty, clinging to her.

'God help us both,' whispered Angel under her breath.

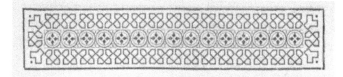

CHAPTER III

THE FIRST DAY

We shall be what you will make us;
　　Make us wise, and make us good!
Make us strong for time of trial,
Teach us temperance, self-denial,
　　Patience, kindness, fortitude!' —MARY HOWITT.

t was, perhaps, just as well that Mr. Crayshaw had to start for London next morning before Godfrey was awake, so that he did not see his young cousin again. He had a talk with Angel, and gave her some money for the housekeeping expenses of the next fortnight, and was a good deal surprised to find how sensible and business-like she could be.

'Cousin Crayshaw really sees how you are beginning to grow up, Angel,' said Betty admiringly, as they came back up the garden path together after seeing their cousin off. 'I wish he talked to me like that. Angel dear, what a lot of money! I don't think that is economy, do you? I should think we might put by a good deal of it for Godfrey to use by-and-bye. Do let's see if we can't save out of it.'

But Angel thought not. She felt she hardly knew enough yet about housekeeping to cut the expenses down lower than her guardian thought fit.

'I must go and talk to Penny,' she said, 'and will you wash the breakfast china and listen for Godfrey moving?'

The breakfast china was a beautiful old set which had been a wedding present to the girls' grandmother, and which Miss Crayshaw in her lifetime had always washed herself, so Betty felt important as she tied on an apron and fetched her hot water.

Angel finished her housekeeping talk and went upstairs to see if Godfrey were still asleep. She opened the bedroom door softly lest she should wake him, but to her surprise he was up and dressed, and kneeling by the bed saying his prayers. He had been taught that at any rate, Angel thought joyfully, and she drew back reverently, not liking to disturb him. But she could not help hearing the last words:

'I will promise to be a very good boy, and if I may not go back to Biddy I would like to go up the ladder to-day, but I should like Biddy best.'

He rose to his feet the next minute and turning his head caught sight of Angel. A half-pleased, half-startled look came over his face.

'Good morning, Godfrey dear,' said his young aunt, coming forward.

The boy put his hands behind him and looked straight at her with his wide grey eyes.

'Good morning,' he said; 'you've come down the ladder for me, I suppose. I like Biddy best, but it can't be helped. Where is the ladder? Are you to go first or am I?'

'What ladder, dear?' said Angelica, dreadfully puzzled.

'What a stupid angel you are!' said the little boy impatiently; 'the ladder you and the others go up and down to Heaven on, of course, like the picture in Biddy's Bible; the ladder you took my papa and mamma up, and Biddy's father, and Corporal O'Roone, and all the others you angels take care of.'

'He must mean Jacob's ladder,' thought Angel. 'I didn't come down that ladder, Godfrey dear,' she said.

Godfrey shook his head.

'I didn't know angels told stories,' he said reproachfully; 'you know you are one, I heard that other call you it.'

'It is only short for my long name,' explained the girl; 'my name is Angelica, Godfrey,—your aunt Angelica, your aunt Angel.'

'I never heard they were aunts,' said Godfrey doubtfully; 'Biddy said just angels.'

'Who is Biddy?' asked Angel, to escape from the difficulty.

'She takes care of me and sometimes of my papa,' said Godfrey readily. 'She takes care of everybody that you angels aren't taking care of. She took care of her father till the angels did it instead, and then she went to church and promised to take care of Corporal O'Roone till the angels got him too. I would rather go back to Biddy, but if I can't I suppose I must go up the ladder with you to my papa.'

It was a queer sort of muddle altogether, and Angel hardly knew whether she felt more like laughing or crying over it. She sat down in the window and drew Godfrey towards her.

'Dear,' she said, 'you have made a mistake. I am not that sort of angel. I hope they take care of you and me and all of us here on earth, as well as where your papa is. But I don't want you to go away. I want you to stay here and be happy with me.'

Godfrey looked at her steadily through his lashes.

'What are you?' he asked abruptly; 'are you a lady?'

'Yes, I think—I hope so,' said Angel.

'Last night I thought you were a white witch, like the ones in Biddy's stories,' said the child, 'and I wanted you to make wings for me. Are you sure, sure you can't? I want to go back.'

His lips began to quiver, and Angel drew him close to her.

'I can't send you back, dear,' she said tenderly; 'couldn't you try to be happy with me? I want to love you very much.'

'Does *he* live here?' asked Godfrey abruptly.

'Cousin Crayshaw do you mean?' asked Angel, in some alarm. 'No; he comes to see us and help us, and tell us what to do.'

'I shall kill him next time he comes,' said Godfrey, calmly; 'I shall hold on to his leg and bite him till he dies.'

'Oh, no, I'm sure you won't!' said Angelica, in dismay; 'no angels will want to be near you, Godfrey, if you wish such unkind things as that.'

'Won't you want to be near me?' asked Godfrey doubtfully.

'I shall be very unhappy,' said Angel, and she added quickly, 'but by-and-bye we can talk about everything. Come down and have breakfast and see your other aunt.'

Godfrey looked at her steadily again for a minute, then he suddenly put his little hand in hers.

'I will go with you,' he said, and Angel kissed him with all her heart and led him downstairs. He was very quiet while he ate his bread-and-milk under the eyes of both aunts, and with Penelope making constant excuses to pop in and out of the room; but his great eyes took note of everything, and now and then he asked some quick question or said decidedly what he liked or did not like. He was very quick, Angel thought, as she watched him, nothing seemed to escape him, and his thoughts flew faster than she could follow. He would be very clever, she said to herself, and her heart failed her a little, for she was not clever, she knew. She was slow at understanding things, afraid of deciding quickly; would she ever be able to guide any one else? She thought about it that afternoon, when Betty had taken her nephew out for a walk and she was busy darning his stockings. They were in dreadful holes, and Angel, as she sat in the parlour window seat with the basket by her side, remembered what she had heard about the way boys wore out their clothes. It made her think of the plans she and Betty used to arrange in their schooldays for mending Bernard's things and taking care of him when he should come home. How little she had dreamt that the mending would be done for Bernard's son! Godfrey had not talked about his father, and Angel had asked no questions and had checked Betty and Penelope. If he should confide in them and tell them about his West Indian home, she would wait and let him do it in his own good time. Just now, everything was strange to him, and she wanted to let him take it in and get used to it all; she could not look for him to love them and be at home with them quite yet. You see, if she was not very quick, she was a very patient person, this Angel; she was content to wait and let her flowers grow, and trust to sun and rain to do the work, without wanting to help by digging them up every day or two to see how the roots looked. And so she sat and thought her gentle thoughts in the creeper-framed window, until she began to wonder where Betty and Godfrey were, and decided to go and meet them. She went down the road, where the wind blew fresh across the common, past one or two cottages, with a word here and there to the children playing at the doors, till she came in sight of the old 'Royal Oak,' the village inn, standing back from the road. In front of the inn was the tree which gave the name both to the house and the village, a noble old oak, hollow inside and propped up with iron supports, but still green above. A tree with a history it was, a tree which could have told many a tale, if it could have spoken, of generations who had passed away, while still its leaves budded fresh and green spring-time after spring-time, and dropped in a russet carpet when the November frosts touched them with cold fingers. But there seemed to be some unusual excitement going on about the oak to-day; a little crowd was collected beneath it: Mr. Collins the innkeeper, and the men and maids, John Ware the miller, pretty Patty Rogers, Nancy's elder sister, Nancy herself, who was always in the forefront when anything was going on, two or three women from the cottages, and, what startled Angel most, Betty, with her shady hat tumbling down her back, gazing up anxiously into the tree, but not Godfrey. Angel quickened her steps and looked where they were looking, and as she drew nearer she heard a chorus of voices.

'Come down, come down, Godfrey, dear Godfrey, you naughty, naughty little boy, come down!'

'Come down, young master; the bough's rotten, 'twon't bear you.'

'Oh, bless him, he'll break his neck, the wood's just tinder! I can't look at him.'

And here Nancy, who loved to have anything, bad or good, to tell, caught sight of Angel and came flying to meet her.

'Oh please, Miss Angelica,' she panted, 'the young gentleman's up the tree and he won't come down nor they can't fetch him, and Mrs. Taylor says he's safe to break his neck, miss—nothing can't save him.'

And then came Betty in a flood of tears.

'Angel, tell him to come down, tell him to come down; he won't listen to me; he'll be killed, he'll be killed!'

'Safe to be!' echoed all the women, as Angel reached the group.

Naughty Godfrey was up the tree in a place that certainly seemed unsafe enough. He was astride upon a bough that did indeed look fearfully rotten, and, though the men below would gladly have gone after him, no one heavier than the slim little boy could have climbed up there in safety.

'The wonder is how he got there, not being a cat,' remarked Ware the miller, who was of a rather dismal turn of mind, 'but he'll want nine lives if he's to get down with a whole skin.'

Angel turned pale as she looked up at him, but she called to him quietly, 'Godfrey, come down at once.'

Godfrey looked down at the sound of her voice, and she thought he looked rather scared.

'I'm going to stop up here,' he said.

'No, you are to come down,' said Angel gravely.

He made a little movement as if he were coming, resting his toe for an instant on a lower bough. As he did so the rotten wood snapped and the branch came down at Angel's feet, leaving Godfrey astride on the bough above, with his feet dangling, while his own seat cracked dangerously. There was a fresh chorus from below.

'The bough's breaking; come down, sir, come down!'

'No, don't move, sir, it'll break if you do; don't stir for your life!'

'Godfrey, keep quite still'—this was from Angel. 'Betty, don't cry; please all of you be quiet, you startle him.'

'Right for you, Miss Angelica,' said the innkeeper; 'hold your tongues, you stupids, if you can. Get into the house and fetch a couple of mattresses and put them here, and look alive about it, will you?'

'You'd best stand a bit back, Miss Angelica,' said the miller, 'else you'll have young master on your head, and there'll be two of you. I'd go up after him if it wouldn't come hard on my wife and six children, one in arms. One must mind one's neck a bit when one's a father, missy.'

'I'd be up after him this minute if the bough'd bear me,' said the innkeeper doubtfully.

Angel answered none of them. She stood still with her white face raised to the little figure in his dangerous position over her head.

He was frightened enough himself now, clinging tightly to the cracking bough and looking fearfully down at the ground beneath him.

'Don't look down, Godfrey,' called Angel encouragingly; 'sit quite still, and we will help you directly.'

At the same moment Peter Rogers came suddenly pushing through the group with a rope in his hand, He said not a word but went up the tree like a squirrel.

''Taint no good, Pete,' the miller began, 'the bough won't bear you.' Angel clutched his coat.

'Be quiet,' she said almost sharply; 'we can't do anything; be quiet.'

Every one obeyed her, and held their breath as Pete climbed to the higher boughs above Godfrey, which, though slender for his weight, looked safer than the dead ones. He fastened the rope where it seemed secure and dropped the end down to the little boy.

'Tie it tight round your waist, young master,' he said; 'tie it in two or three knots.'

Those below would have given directions too, but Angel stopped them again.

'Hush! let Pete tell him; don't confuse him.'

There was dead silence again, while Godfrey, looking up at Peter, struggled with his little fingers over the stiff rope. The maids came out while he was doing it, and, at their master's sign, put down the mattresses silently under the tree.

'Now come back, sir,' said Peter from above. 'Mind, you can't fall, the rope's tight, and I'll have you in a minute. Don't look down, and come along gently.'

His quiet voice seemed to give Godfrey confidence and he obeyed, pushing himself along the bough. Betty hid her face against Angel, and squeezed her sister's fingers till they were hot and sore. The miller puffed with excitement and began to say something, when the innkeeper clapped his big hand over his mouth. It did not really last a minute, but it seemed an hour before Peter, standing firm in a fork of the tree, could reach the child and drag him towards him, even as the branch on which Godfrey had been sitting crashed down on to the mattress at Angelica's feet. Another minute, and Peter was helping the little boy down the tree, amid a chorus of congratulation from below. Every one had something to say, some comment to make, except Angel, who just took tight hold of Godfrey's hand, as he stood quite quiet, hanging his head in the midst. She checked Betty with a gentle touch when she would have seized hold of him, though she was wanting dreadfully to hug him herself.

'Thank you all very much,' she said softly, to the people round her. 'I think we will go home now; come, Godfrey.' And she led him away with Betty following. After a minute or two she said:

'Godfrey, you have given us a most terrible fright. We must be very thankful you were not killed.'

'The other angels saw to me,' said Godfrey.

'Yes, but we mustn't look for angels to take care of us when we go into dangerous places where we have no business to be. Why did you climb the tree, Godfrey?'

'Because she said I couldn't,' said Godfrey stoutly.

'Do you mean your Aunt Elizabeth? It was very naughty of you to do what she told you not. We must take you home now and leave you with Penny because we can't trust you.'

All the time her kind heart was aching over the terribleness of having to be severe with him on the very first day, the longing to catch him up and kiss him and cry over him. But she kept on saying to herself, 'We must—we must, there is nobody else to do it,' and so she managed to be firm. She took Godfrey home, talked to him tenderly and gravely, and left him in the little room where Penny sat sewing. She felt as if she had not said half she meant, as if she had made a thousand mistakes, though she had tried her very best to be wise. Godfrey had listened silently to all she said; he would think about it, Angel hoped, and perhaps by-and-bye he would say something; she must just wait. Then she went to find her sister. Betty had not come into the house, and Angel, going out to look for her, heard sounds of sobbing by the arbour. Everything Betty did was always done vehemently, and there she was now, lying full length on the grass, with her head on Demoiselle Jehanne's stone shoulder, crying as if her heart would break.

'Betty dear, don't lie there, the grass is damp,' said Angelica, leaning over her. Betty left Miss Jane to throw her arms round her sister.

'Oh, Angel,' she sobbed, 'I can't—I can't ever be it! It's no use, I can't be a maiden aunt, I know I never shall. This first day, this very first, he's nearly killed himself. Oh, Angel, if I shut my eyes, I can see him with his darling neck broken, and the funeral, and Cousin Crayshaw coming down to it and looking "I told you so." And perhaps wicked people, who might think we want his money, might say we planned it, like the Babes in the Wood's uncle, and there might be a trial, and you and me tried for making away with Bernard's little boy.'

'Betty, Betty,' gasped Angel, who never could follow the pace of Betty's imagination, 'don't say such dreadful things! Godfrey's quite safe, and I'm sure you couldn't help it.'

'That's the worst of it, I couldn't help it,' sobbed Betty; 'I can't make him do as I tell him, and he won't—he won't—he won't call me Aunt Elizabeth,' and she watered Miss Jane's convolvulus with fresh tears.

'I am thinking,' said Angel hesitatingly, 'that perhaps we expected a little too much to begin with; you see, we had had no practice before, so perhaps it is natural we should make a few mistakes.'

'But we don't want to practise on Godfrey,' wailed Betty, 'and, if he gets killed while we're learning, where will be the use of us getting wise about it? Fancy us left to get quite old, two wise maiden aunts with no nephew to be aunt to, and all Godfrey's dreadful money for our own, and people thinking we liked it.'

The picture was altogether too dreadful for Angel to fancy at all.

'Don't you think perhaps it's better not to think about such dreadful things happening?' she said hesitatingly; 'and Betty, do you know, I've just remembered that I don't think we half thanked Pete properly. Shall we go down to the Place and see if we can find him?'

'I think we'd better,' said Betty, rising; 'I'm sure I ought, for he's saved Godfrey's neck from being broken, and me from either dying of a broken heart or going quite mad. Fancy if you'd had to live alone, Angel, or to come and see me in an asylum, perhaps talk to me through bars. Yes, I think we'd better go and thank Pete.'

Angelica put her sister's tangled curls straight and tied on her hat, and they went together rather slowly and mournfully down the road to Oakfield Place.

They were quite at home there, and went in through the garden to the back of the house, where Patty was feeding chickens in the orchard with Nancy helping her. Nancy came running to meet the young ladies, stopping in dismay at sight of Betty's tear-stained face, and Patty asked anxiously if the young gentleman were hurt.

'Oh no, not at all, thank you,' said Angel, 'only he frightened us a good deal. Is Peter in, Patty? We wanted to thank him for being so sensible and helping Godfrey so cleverly.'

Pete would be in directly, Patty thought; he had just gone to the mill, he was bound to be back soon. Mother was making the lavender bags in the storeroom, wouldn't the young ladies step in? she'd be fine and pleased; and she showed them into the house and held back Nancy, who would have followed, since she never would learn when she wasn't wanted. The store-room was a long, low room, running along the back of the house and looking on to the garden. To-day it was full of the clean, pleasant scent of lavender; there were great trays of dried lavender on the long table, and Martha Rogers sat stitching away at muslin bags to put it in. Every year those lavender bags were made at Oakfield Place; they were all alike, of black muslin bound with lilac-coloured ribbon. Old Mrs. Maitland had made them herself up to the last year she lived; there were great stores of beautiful linen in the house, sheets and towels and table-cloths which she and her sisters had stitched at in their young days, and they were all stowed away in big presses, with the fragrant lavender between them, until the captain should bring a wife home to Oakfield and want them. The lavender bags which she did not use herself Mrs. Maitland gave to her friends; there was no one she had been fond of who did not possess several of the little sweet-scented presents. Miss Amelia Crayshaw had had plenty of them, and Angel and Betty had received one each, long ago, one day when they had been to drink tea at the Place with their cousin before Mrs. Maitland died. And as long as they lived the scent of lavender would always bring back to them the old house, and the sunny sloping garden, and the long, low store-room, with its deep window seats and shelves and presses, and Martha stitching away at black muslin and lilac ribbon. For the captain liked to know that things were done still as they had been in his mother's lifetime, and so the lavender was gathered every year, and the bags were made to put among the stores of linen which was waiting, all snowy and fragrant, till the master of the house came home.

Martha Rogers was a tall, comely woman, with capable hands and a sensible motherly face. And, indeed, she had mothered and cosseted many a child besides her own three, and Angel and Betty Wyndham were among the number. Often and often when they were little girls they had come to Martha with their troubles, for Cousin Amelia, though she was always kind, seemed to have forgotten the long ago time when she was a child, when little things looked so big, and a broken doll or a wet birthday made all the world dark for a little while. And Penny, though she was quite ready to pet and comfort them, never had very much to suggest except kisses and sugar and a bit of cake. But Martha Rogers, though she was so big and wise and busy, had that beautiful power, which we must all learn if we are going to be helpful, sympathizing people, of remembering what it was like to be little and shy and stupid, and never talked about it being a waste of time and tears to cry over playthings, or thought that people could be comforted by sweetmeats and advice not to spoil their pretty eyes. There was a sort of strong, happy feeling about her very presence, and Angel and Betty felt it to-day as they came into the lavender-scented store-room. Martha gave them a hearty welcome as usual.

'Come in, Miss Angel, come in, Miss Betty dear; 'tis a while since I saw you. Sit ye down here, Miss Angel, out of the draught. Bless your heart, my dear, where are your roses? But, of course, Patty's just told me the fright you've got about the young gentleman—a little Turk, to be sure; but there, boys will be boys, won't they, and never easy till they're in mischief one way or the other.'

Angel began to answer her, and then suddenly, at the kind hearty words, her composure broke down, and she dropped her face in her hands and cried as Betty had done.

'It's my fault, Martha,' faltered Betty, in explanation, 'it was me he was with, and I couldn't stop him doing it. And he's got nobody but us to look to, you know, and how are we ever going to teach him?'

Martha Rogers looked from one of the sisters to the other, and then she stuck her needle into the black muslin and came over to

Angelica, and began stroking her bowed head with her broad tender hand.

'Poor dears! poor little ladies!' she said gently; 'bless your hearts, my dears, if you take on like this every time the young gentleman takes a frolic you'll have your hair white before you're twenty.'

'But, Martha,' sighed Betty, 'you know he did what I told him not to do.'

'Ay, did he, Miss Betty dear; and many's the time, I doubt, he'll take his own way again, like the rest of us, and be sorry for it, sure enough.'

'But if I can't make him obey me,' said Betty dolefully, 'there's nobody but us, you know.'

'Miss Betty dear, not all the King's army and navy can't make the smallest bit of a child obey them if he won't. You can tell a child what's right and punish him if he does wrong, but you can't make him do what you want, like you can drive a nail into a board. I'll warrant you've told him he's been a bad boy and put you both about, and scared everybody.'

'Yes, I told him,' said Angel, lifting her face, 'but, Martha, I don't know if he minded.'

'He'll mind by-and-bye, if he didn't then, Miss Angelica, and be worse vexed to think he's hurt you than to have nigh broken his neck.'

Angel looked gravely up at her.'

'Martha,' she said simply, 'you are always so good to us, and you know we have to be everything to Godfrey, and we have no one else to ask, so you will tell me what you think. Of course we want Godfrey to obey us for love—it would break my heart if he didn't love us—but still he must be punished if he does wrong, and there is no one else to do it. Sha'n't we find it very hard to make him care for us, and yet treat him rightly and wisely?'

Martha Rogers sat down again in the chair where she had been stitching the lavender bags, but she did not take up her work. She smoothed her large apron down thoughtfully once or twice and then she began to speak slowly, looking beyond Angel out of the window.

'You'll pardon me, Miss Angelica, I'm only just one that's been a child myself and seen myself over again in my own children, but this is how it seems to me. I think when we're bits of boys and girls, before we've learnt much of how other folks do things, the Lord gives us a very good notion of what's fair and right, and we look to see older folks have the same. When I was a young wife, Miss Angel, and Patty yonder was in her cradle, my grannie, that brought me up, said much the same thing to me. "Martha," says she, "yon little lass'll meet a many unfair things, and a many contrairy things to puzzle her before she's a grown woman; don't let her meet 'em in her mother, my dear. Let her have some one she can hold on to, and reckon on to blame her when she's wrong and praise her when she's right. If she breaks your best jug by accident don't go for to scold her, but if she takes a bit of sugar on the sly ye may take the birch to her." If young master's like most of the little lads I've known, Miss Angel, he'll put them first that loves him well enough to put what's fair before what's pleasant for him or for them.'

'But, Martha,' said Angel earnestly, 'you were older than we are, and you had your grannie to ask, and we are so afraid of making mistakes.'

'Miss Angelica, you'll forgive me for what I'm going to say. I'm not making light, missy dear, but what can you do more than do your best, and show him what's right and punish him when he's wrong, and say your prayers for him, and love him all you can; but remember all the time that there's One wiser than you loves him better still.'

42

And here Martha took up the lavender bag and began stitching away at the lilac ribbon binding. But she had to leave off after a minute, for Betty sprang up suddenly and put her arms round her neck and kissed her, and Angel looked at her across the table with earnest, grateful eyes.

'Thank you, Martha, so very much,' she said; 'you do help us so beautifully, better than any one else could!'

'I just tell you what I told myself, Miss Angel dear, and, mind you, my dear young ladies, I don't believe we've ever a job given us to do but we're taught the way, so we really want to learn.'

Just at this moment Peter came in from the mill, and the two young ladies thanked him till he got red to the tips of his ears. It was nothing at all to do, he said, and he was glad the young master was none the worse, and a first-rate climber he was, that he was, and him such a little bit of a fellow. And so the girls went away, very much more cheerful than they had come.

'We won't say any more about it to Godfrey,' Angelica said on the way home; 'it's just as Martha says, we can't make him say he's sorry, and if he is he'll tell us so by-and-bye, and it'll be worth waiting for, won't it?'

So the two waited, and in the evening they had their reward. Angelica put Godfrey to bed and heard him say his prayers, adding herself a few words of thanksgiving for his preservation that day. When she leaned over him to say good-night, he asked in his sudden way:

'If I had tumbled down and my head had been broken off would you have cried?'

'Indeed I should,' said Angel gravely; 'I am afraid to think about it even.'

'But I wasn't a good boy then,' went on Godfrey, with his wide grey eyes studying her face; 'are you going on loving me?'

'My little Godfrey, I shall go on loving you as long as I live, and longer, longer, dear.'

The next moment he put his arms round her and gave her his first real kiss.

'I love you,' he said gravely; 'I won't make you and the other angels cry. You can tell the other one, the Aunt Betty, that I won't climb up that tree again.'

'Yes, that I will,' Angel said joyfully, and she went downstairs to the parlour where Betty was reading and Penny clearing away supper, with her quiet face glowing with happiness.

'Betty,' she said, 'Godfrey is quite sorry now for frightening us. He told me to tell you that he wouldn't do it again.'

'Bless him!' exclaimed Penny, almost dropping the lamp.

'Darling!' cried Betty, letting her book tumble into the fender. 'Angel, did he—did he say "Aunt Elizabeth"?'

'Well, no,' said Angel, picking the book up and dusting off the ashes; 'but, Betty, do you know, I think perhaps we'd better not make a fuss about that if he thinks the other sounds nicer; if we're too strict about little things we sha'n't know what to do about big ones, I think.'

'I thought perhaps he'd find "Aunt Elizabeth" easier to respect,' said Betty a little regretfully.

'I think he'll respect the person and not mind about the name,' said Angel, and she added thoughtfully, looking into the fire, 'I really mind more about my own name, because I'm afraid he mixes me up with what he has learnt about guardian angels, but I must just wait, and he'll find out his mistake all in good time.'

Old Penny was carrying the supper tray out of the room, and, as she stopped to shut the door after her, she remarked to herself:

'Bless your heart, my dear, if young master makes no worse mistakes than that in his life he won't go far wrong!'

CHAPTER IV

A HEART OF OAK

'For a-fighting we must go,
And a-fighting we must go,
And what's the odds if you lose your legs,
So long as you drub the foe?'

t was Sunday afternoon, the fourth Sunday after Godfrey's coming to Oakfield. It was almost the end of October now, but the spell of warm weather which we call St. Luke's summer had come, as it often does in late autumn, and the sun was warm and pleasant as Angelica paced up and down the garden path with a book in her hand. Mr. Crayshaw sat in the sunny parlour window where Angel's work-basket stood on week-days; he, too, had a book before him, but I'm afraid he was nodding over it, for there was a sleepy quiet about the house that afternoon. Only at the bottom of the garden by the arbour voices could be heard, and Angel caught a word or two every time she reached the end of the gravel walk, words that mingled strangely with the book of poetry she was reading.

'Be useful where thou livest, that they may
Both want and wish thy pleasing presence still,'

read Angel as she strolled along the path. Then came Betty's clear tones from behind the yew hedge which separated her from the arbour:

'Now, Godfrey, say after me: "To love, honour, and succour my father and mother."'

'No, Aunt Betty, I needn't learn that. Penny says we oughtn't ever to waste precious time, and I hav'n't any papa and mamma to succour, so it's waste of time to learn about succouring them.'

'No, Godfrey, it isn't; because it means any one that stands in the place of a papa and mamma to you, your relations and friends that take care of you.'

'Aunts?' inquired Godfrey.

'Yes, certainly aunts.'

'Cousins?' asked Godfrey, with much unwillingness in his tone. Angel had turned round again before Betty's answer came. She was rather glad the question had not been put to her. Godfrey always would have his inquiries answered, and Angel felt sure he would not like to be told that it was his duty to succour Cousin Crayshaw. She paced up the gravel path and back again with her head bent over her book.

'Scorn no man's love, though of a mean degree,
Love is a present for a mighty king.'

She had got so far when she reached the arbour again, and this time there was a shadow of impatience in Betty's tones.

'Godfrey, you are not attending. "Not to covet nor desire other men's goods."'

'What are goods?'

'Things that belong to them. If you wanted my desk or Cousin Crayshaw's watch it would be naughty of you. Godfrey, you must not put your foot on Miss Jane's head; her nose is off already.'

'I don't want his watch, I want a much bigger one. Aunt Betty, was that lady as ugly when she was alive as she is now?'

'Godfrey, that isn't a kind thing to say. People have been cruel to her—you wouldn't be pretty if your nose was off; and besides, she is dead, and it isn't right to speak so about her.'

'What killed her?' asked Godfrey gravely.

'Well, of course, we don't know for certain, but your Aunt Angelica and I feel almost sure she died young. You see she was *Miss* Jane, she wasn't married, and we have always had an idea that she died of a broken heart.'

'What broke it?' said Godfrey's interested voice.

'Of course I don't know for certain; but she was a maiden, you see— 'demoiselle' means a maiden—and she may have been a maiden aunt—there's no reason why she shouldn't have been—and her nephew may have broken her heart by his bad ways.'

'What did he do?' asked Godfrey earnestly.

'It may have been what he didn't do,' said Betty impressively. 'Not learning things that were for his good, and—and that sort of thing.'

'When people's hearts break do you hear them crack?' was the next question.

'No, you don't hear anything,' said Betty solemnly; 'the people get paler and paler and thinner and thinner every day, till at last they die.'

'You ar'n't thin, Aunt Betty,' remarked the nephew, with satisfaction.

'Not now, perhaps,' said the aunt, with dignity, 'but I might soon get thin with lying awake thinking sad things about little boys.'

'Do you lie awake thinking of me not learning about succouring you and Cousin Crayshaw?'

'I haven't yet,' said Betty truthfully; 'but I soon might,' she hastened to add.

'I'll say it again now,' said Godfrey after a moment, 'and afterwards will you tell me about godpapa Godfrey and the acorn?'

'Yes, of course I will,' and then, as 'My duty to my neighbour' began again, Angel turned away with a smile in her gentle eyes.

Certainly in these three weeks the two young aunts had managed to win their little nephew's confidence. It had not come quite directly, for poor Godfrey was not one of those lucky little children who grow up with the happy belief that every one is friendly to them, and so open their glad hearts to all the world. Bit by bit they had learned the story of his short little life which there was no one but himself to tell them. His mother was only a name to him, and he knew little about his father, who was always kind, Godfrey said, but hardly ever saw him. He didn't talk, the child told Angel; he took him on his knee sometimes and looked at him, and Angel's gentle, pitiful heart drew its own pictures, and fancied her brother mourning for his young wife, estranged from his relations at home, perhaps afraid to cling too closely to what was left him. Biddy O'Roone, the corporal's widow, was evidently the chief person in Godfrey's world. Godfrey had been ill once, he said; he couldn't remember much about it, but Biddy came and sent away his black nurse, and after that she took care of him. She taught him what she could, to speak the truth and say his prayers morning and evening, and he was obedient to her, though the soldiers and the native servants did their best to spoil him. She could not read herself, but she knew most of the Bible stories, and Godfrey learnt them from hearing her tell them, and imagined all kinds of things about them afterwards. And she told him, too, endless fairy stories about witches and enchanters, and the good folk who danced at night on the greenswards at home. One of the soldiers taught him a little reading and writing, and another taught him to talk some French, and though he was small and delicate he had plenty of true English pluck and spirit, and would ride or climb against a boy twice his age.

It was Biddy who had awakened him one night when his papa was away from home, and had dressed him in a hurry, and told him that he was to be quiet and come away with her at once, for there were rascals about that hadn't a bit of pity in the black hearts of them for old or young. And Godfrey, half asleep and not understanding, was hurried away in the dark and found himself presently on board ship. And when, next day, he asked where his papa was, Biddy cried over him and told him in her simple way that the angels had taken him. And Godfrey had been a little sorry, but had supposed he would just stay on with Biddy, and by-and-bye they got to a great place full of houses where she had friends, and he thought it was America. And, not long afterwards, she mended his clothes and knitted some stockings for him, and told him that he was going to England, to some grand relations whose name was in his papa's pocket book, and that her heart was just breaking with joy for him being made a lovely gentleman, as indeed he should be, if it wasn't just broken entirely with sorrow to think how would she ever get on and the seas between them.

He had learnt among his soldier friends that it was unmanly to cry or make a fuss before people, and so his fellow travellers, who might have petted the delicate-looking little boy, set him down as rather sulky and stupid. He arrived in England on a dull rainy day, which seemed terrible to the little West Indian boy, and then came Cousin Crayshaw with his grave disapproving face and stiff manner, and Godfrey felt as if he must die if he could not get away and back to Biddy directly. That was what had made him so disobedient on the journey down from London, and when he arrived, tired and cold and bewildered, at Oakfield Cottage, he felt as if he must get away now or never. It was then that the sight of Angel, and the idea that she was a sort of fairy, had given him the wild hope that she might help him, and when that hope failed him there seemed to be nothing left but to pray that the angels might take him, as they had taken his papa and mamma, away from the strange, dreadful world. Then Angelica's sweetness and gentleness had begun to win the little lonely heart, and his disobedience to Betty on the first day had been a bit of perversity, just to show that he was not going to give in all at once. But when Godfrey gave his heart he gave it for good and all, and after that evening when he first kissed Angel he held out no longer, and soon made himself as much at home at Oakfield as if he had lived there all his life. He was a good deal like Betty herself in some things, just as bright and quick and fanciful, making up his mind about everything directly, and liking or disliking with all his might. Angel used to listen to them in wonder, as Godfrey asked torrents of questions and Betty answered them as readily as possible, and they went on supposing this and supposing that much faster than she could follow. Godfrey was quite different with her, much quieter and gentler, and Angel thought it very kind of him to wait, looking patiently up into her face while she thought things out and talked to him in her careful, deliberate way; and she feared he must think her stupid, and that would be so bad for him. She was a little bit afraid, too, that he was not even now quite clear about the difference between herself and the angels who watched over him, for he was apt to get confused between true stories and fairy stories and his own imaginings. One day she just hinted at it to Martha Rogers, but Martha didn't think it mattered. She advised Angel not to bother herself and little master too much about small things, which would get clear to him by-and-bye: children thought a many queer things which did no harm. And to herself she said, as Penelope had done, that if Godfrey made no worse mistakes than confusing his gentle young aunt with his angel guardians he would not go very far wrong. And Angel, feeling sure Martha knew best, was content to wait and not trouble about it. If Betty could have found a fault in her elder sister's dealings with their nephew it would have been that she was not strict and particular enough about what she called details. Betty wanted to bring up Godfrey on a proper plan, and she had arranged a set of rules which were all very excellent, only she changed them so often. She would waken her sister in the middle of the night with the eager exclamation, 'Angel dear, I beg your pardon for disturbing you, but don't you think we should begin at once teaching Godfrey to dance? It is such an excellent exercise you know, and I thought I might give him an hour every morning after breakfast, when he generally goes in the garden while you're talking to Penny.'

And Angel would say, in a rather sleepy voice,

'But, Betty dear, what about washing the china?'

And Betty would start off at once on a new set of arrangements to fit in everything.

Or she would burst into the kitchen with another idea, while Angelica was ordering the dinner.

'Angel dear, don't you think it would be very healthy for Godfrey to live entirely on vegetables? In that paper Cousin Crayshaw brought down it said it was such a capital thing for children. He might begin on potatoes to-day, and to-morrow he might have vegetable marrow, and we might draw up a list for every day in the week.'

It was all rather distracting to Angel, who felt quite sure that Betty was much cleverer than she was, and yet dreaded trying any experiment with Godfrey which she did not quite understand. It was Betty's idea that Godfrey should spend Sunday afternoon in learning his Catechism; all children learnt their Catechism on a Sunday, she said, and the sooner Godfrey began the better. Besides, once a month the children were catechized in church, and she didn't want him to be behind Nancy Rogers and Jerry Ware, and all the village boys and girls. So he said the answers after her and she explained them, which she certainly did very brightly and very well, and on week-days Angel taught him the earlier ones, in her gentle, plodding way, till he knew them by heart. He had done what his Aunt Betty required of him by the time Angel had taken two more turns, and was having his reward in the story which he called godpapa and the acorn. It was his favourite of all Betty's tales, and it was the sort she liked best to tell, with a little bit of fact and a great deal of imagining. Certainly there was not very much fact to begin upon, only an old tradition of one of William the Conqueror's barons, who had long ago owned land at Oakfield and had planted the tree which gave the place its name. What chiefly interested

Godfrey was that the baron of the oak had borne the same Christian name as himself, though nobody knew his surname.

'Was that why they called me that?' he asked eagerly, the first time Betty told him the story.

Betty could not say for certain, but she and Angel had fancied that Godfrey's father, who had been at Oakfield often when he was a little boy, might have been thinking of his English home when he chose the name, for he had no relation called Godfrey. At any rate Betty and her nephew decided that it must have been so, and when Godfrey came to godparents in the Catechism and did not know who his own had been, he christened the great Norman baron 'godpapa,' and loved to sit at Betty's feet with his chin on her knee, looking up with his wide grey eyes into hers, while she told how well the gallant Sir Godfrey had fought at Hastings, and how the king had given him the wide stretch of fair pasture and forest as a reward for his valour, and how perhaps the acorn was the very first thing he planted, and how his wife liked to come out on a summer evening and mark how it grew into a young tree, and how his grandchildren and great-grandchildren played under its shadow.

'And did he sit under it when it was a big tree?' asked Godfrey in his earnest way.

'Well, no, I don't think he could have himself, because, you see, by that time he must have been dead and buried in the church — very likely close by Miss Jane, with his figure all in armour on the top, and a little dog at his feet.'

'No, but I would rather have him sitting under the oak,' persisted Godfrey; 'make it a different end, Auntie Betty,' and as Angelica came round the end of the yew hedge, he ran to meet her, exclaiming,

'Auntie Angel, make Auntie Betty make godpapa Godfrey sit under his own tree.'

Angel sat down and drew him to her side, while Betty repeated:

'I can't, Godfrey, because it wouldn't be real. I told you he couldn't be alive when it was a big tree, unless he got as old as the people at the beginning of the Bible.'

'You see, Godfrey dear,' began Angel in her quiet way, 'it is often like that with the good things people do; they don't get all the good of them themselves, but somebody else, perhaps ever so long after, is the happier for what they have done. I think it is rather nice to think of our dear old oak being green and shady year after year, and reminding us that the man who planted it so long ago helped to make Oakfield a little prettier. You know everything that God puts into the world, animals and plants, and even little flowers and insects, they are all useful somehow, though we don't always see how, and so men and women, who can think and plan and work, ought to do something besides just enjoying themselves, they ought to leave some mark of their having been here.'

Godfrey's eyes drank in every word.

'Are you doing something, Aunt Angel?' he asked gravely.

Angel flushed her pretty pink.

'I can't do very much, Godfrey,' she said; 'I should like to make people a little happier, and then, you know, I want you to do a great deal, and your Aunt Betty and I are trying to teach you what we can to help you: that is like Sir Godfrey planting the oak tree, and hoping that one day it would be beautiful for every one to see.'

Godfrey leaned hard with both elbows on her knee.

'What useful things shall I do?' he asked.

'I don't know; we shall see by-and-bye. I should try and make every one very happy now, if I were you, and learn all I could, so that when you are a man, and can help more people, you may have the power and the wisdom you want.'

'Only think if you were a great scholar,' put in Betty, 'and wrote a book—no, a lot of books, and people had them in their libraries, all bound the same, and with "By Godfrey Wyndham" on the back. Or,' as Godfrey looked only doubtfully pleased, 'if you were a great statesman and made speeches, or suppose you were a soldier and beat the French.'

'Would that be useful?' asked Godfrey of Angel.

'Yes, certainly, very useful if the French were coming to conquer England.'

'Pete is useful, isn't he?' said Godfrey; 'Penny says he's the usefullest man about the place. Perhaps I might be a useful gardener, Auntie Betty; I should like that, and I could plant lots of things then to come up for other people; or couldn't I be a useful miller like Ware? because people must have bread, and I should like a mill.'

'But why can't you be a statesman or a general?' said Betty, rather taken aback.

'I would rather be a gardener like Pete,' persisted Godfrey; 'why can't I? Gardeners are useful.'

'I think,' said Angel, 'because it isn't the state of life into which it has pleased God to call you, Godfrey dear, like the Catechism you were learning. We can't choose always just what we should like to be, we have to do our best just where we are put.'

'It's getting cold,' said Betty, springing up; 'shall we go down to the Place and see if the cow that was ill is any better? There's time before supper.' So the aunts and the nephew strolled down the road together, forgetting, for the present, the subject of Godfrey's future profession. And none of them guessed how much that Sunday afternoon call would do towards deciding it. When they reached the gate of Oakfield Place, Nancy came running to meet them, brimful of news as usual.

'Oh, please, Miss Angelica, oh, please, Miss Elizabeth,' she began—for though Godfrey wouldn't use his aunts' long names himself, Peter always strictly obeyed Betty's wishes and made Nancy do the same—'oh, please, Uncle Kiah's come. He came last night, and the Frenchmen have got his leg and two of his fingers, and the captain is going to get him some money from the King and he's to live here always; and he'd have been at church this morning only he isn't just right used to his new leg, and he was afraid he'd tumble down before all the folks in church and give the parson a start, so he thought he'd wait till next Sunday.'

'Do you mean your sailor uncle, Nancy?' asked Betty eagerly as Nancy paused for breath.

'Yes, miss, Uncle Hezekiah Parker; please come in, miss, he tells such rare stories, miss.'

'But, Nancy, perhaps your mother won't want us to-day, just now when your uncle's come home,' said Angel.

'Oh, yes, miss, she will, please Miss Angel—Miss Angelica—and so will Uncle Kiah too. He's here, miss,' and Nancy ushered her visitors to the back of the house, where the kitchen and store-room windows looked out. There was quite a Sunday air about the place; William Rogers and Pete, in their best clothes, were looking at the cows in the orchard, while Patty was gathering some cabbages to feed them. Martha was moving about in the kitchen and singing a quiet, sleepy psalm tune to herself, and on the sunny bench under the window sat a brisk-looking, white-haired old man with a wooden leg, beating time to the psalm tune with the stick in his hand. When he caught sight of the young ladies he jumped up directly and made quite a grand bow, though Angel almost caught hold of him, she was so afraid he would tumble over.

'How do you do, Hezekiah?' she said; 'we're so glad to see you. We've been so sorry to hear about your—about your—misfortunes.'

'None at all, missy, none at all worth speaking of,' said the old sailor cheerily, balancing himself with his stick; 'the Frenchies have got my old leg, and much good may it do 'em. The old neighbours have been in, making a deal o' fuss over me, but I tells 'em to keep their pity for them that wants it more, and I've one less leg for the rheumaticks to get hold of,' and the old sailor laughed at his own joke like a storm of wind in the rigging.

'And now you've come to settle down at Oakfield?' said Angelica.

'Ay, ay, miss, thanks to the captain, the best officer that ever trod quarter-deck, bless his heart. A hot time he'll be giving the "froggies," I'll warrant him, so he and the old *Mermaid* be getting any work to do.'

'I'm afraid you'll find it rather dull here after where you've been,' said Betty.

'Not I, missy,' was the cheery answer; 'places is much as you makes 'em all the world over, and it's fair and right the old hulk should put into port and see the young craft putting out. I'll find enough to keep me from rusting, never you fear.'

'My nephew, Master Godfrey, likes stories better than anything,' said Angel, putting the little boy forward; 'will you tell him about some of the things you have seen, while I talk to Martha?'

Godfrey had been watching the sailor with earnest eyes all the time he talked, and now he came up readily and sat down on the bench beside him; Betty, who was devoted to animals, ran down to ask after the cows and coax them with cabbages, and Angelica went to Martha in the kitchen. A woman in the village was ill, and she wanted to consult Martha about what to take to her. It took a good time to talk it over, and when she came out again the twilight was deepening. Hezekiah still sat on the bench outside, and Betty was sitting by him, while Pete, Patty, Nancy, and their father stood silently listening. As for Godfrey he sat as if he had not moved since she left him, and his eyes never left the sailor's face, except to glance at what the old man was drawing on the ground with his stick, the line of the ships in a great sea-fight. Long afterwards Angel remembered it all, as one goes back to scenes which seemed of no importance at the time but were really the beginning of great events—the autumn evening, with the damp heavy scent on the air, the white mist clinging to the low ground, while above the sky cleared for a starry night, the late monthly roses on the house, the old sailor and his little group of listeners.

'Godfrey,' she said softly, 'it is time to go home.'

The little boy started and drew a long breath.

'Bless him, he ain't here,' chuckled old Kiah; 'he's off the Spanish coast, missy, along o' Lord Nelson and our captain. You come again, young master, and I'll tell you the rest.' And then he would hobble himself to the gate to let them out. 'Never tell me,' he said, as Pete hurried to do it instead and Patty to give him her arm, 'I'm not quite useless yet, no more I am; I told the captain he'd find me doing a hand's turn when he came home. I've got one leg and a hand and a half the Frenchies left me, and I'll make something of them if I'm not much mistaken.'

All the way home Betty talked eagerly about the old sailor, where he had been, what he had seen, the great men he had known. Godfrey said not a word and asked no questions, and yet Angel was sure he thought of nothing else all the evening. But he told none of his thoughts until just before he was going to say his prayers. Then he said suddenly:

'Aunt Angel, that man is a very useful man; he must have been the usefullest man that could be when his leg was on.'

Then, leaning on her lap as he did when he was excited, he went on:

'When you want something, you ask God for it, don't you, Aunt Angel?'

'We ask that we may have it if God pleases,' said Angel reverently.

'Yes,' said Godfrey, 'and I am going to ask, if it pleases Him, to call me into the state of being a useful sailor.'

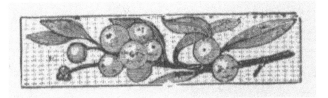

CHAPTER V

THE WRONG END

'You won't say, what is it I want? but, what is it I've got to
do? What have I got to do or to bear, and how can I do it or
bear it best? That's the only safe point to make for, my lad;
make for it and leave the rest.'—J. H. EWING.

or the next few days Betty and her nephew
spent most of their spare time on Hezekiah's
bench under the kitchen window at the Place.
Betty talked of nothing but naval battles, but
Godfrey still said very little, and after that
Sunday night never spoke again of being a
sailor. Angel wondered, for it was not like
Godfrey, who generally had plenty to say; but she noticed
sometimes, when Betty was telling Kiah Parker's stories, that
Godfrey's face took that strange resolute set that surprised her so
much when he first came. It gave her new ideas about her little
nephew, and showed her that, under all his liveliness and fancy,
there was a strong will which it would be very hard to alter if once
he made up his mind. It frightened her a little, for she did not feel
half wise enough to lead him to make up his mind the right way. She
did not talk to Betty about it; indeed at present Betty's head seemed
too full of ships to hold anything else. Hezekiah had made Godfrey a
beautiful little model vessel, carpentering quite wonderfully with his
remaining fingers, and had taught him the names of the ropes, which
the boy learnt directly. That was all very well, but when it came to
his saying them over to Betty when he ought to have been doing his
reading lesson, and drawing little ships on the slate when he should
have been at his sums, Angel began to be rather alarmed, and

ventured to speak gently to her sister about Godfrey's neglecting his lessons. Betty was always ready enough to own herself in the wrong; she was overwhelmed with penitence before Angel had half finished her gentle remonstrance.

'I declare I want looking after twenty times more than Godfrey does,' she exclaimed, with the quick tears in her bright eyes. 'I won't go near Kiah for a week, and no more shall he.'

'Oh no, you mustn't do that!' exclaimed Angelica, in dismay; 'that wouldn't be fair to poor Kiah or Godfrey either. I like you to go there. I think it is a good thing; only I don't think it ought to interfere with other things that have to be done.'

Betty stopped her as usual with a vehement hug.

'You are, next to Martha, the wisest person in the world, Angel. It's Godfrey's history lesson this morning, and I'll take care we both do it properly.'

But Betty had to find out that it is easier to make resolutions for ourselves than to impress them upon other people. Godfrey was by no means inclined for his history lesson that morning. Betty had taken a great deal of trouble to understand about the Norman Conquest herself, and to make it easy for Godfrey, but he would not take any interest to-day in the oppression of the poor Saxons, or the curfew bell, or Domesday Book.

'I want to go back to them coming over,' he persisted. 'What was his flag-ship like—the admiral's I mean?'

'If you mean William the Conqueror's I don't know, and he wasn't an admiral, he was a general. Godfrey, don't look out of the window—what are you thinking about?'

'I'm thinking that if the Channel Fleet had watched the harbours properly those French ships wouldn't ever have got out of port.'

'Godfrey, you must attend to what I am telling you. Now then, what was the curfew?'

'A bird with a long beak that squeals; Kiah says — —'

Betty rose up majestically.

'Godfrey, if you think it is funny to pretend that you think I said curlew you are very much mistaken. I have a very great many things to do, more things than a little boy like you can count, and I can't spend all the morning with you. So I am going to write on this slate: "The curfew bell was rung at eight o'clock every night as a sign that people were to put their lights out and go to bed," and you are to go on copying it and copying it till the slate is quite full.'

Godfrey said not a word, only watched while Betty wrote the words in a bold round hand, and ruled double lines with a decided sweep of her slate pencil, and then walked out of the room with her most 'maiden aunt' expression. But when she was gone I am sorry to say that he got on a chair, reached down his wooden ship from its high shelf, climbed out of the window into the garden, and went out through a gate in the fence and across the fields. He was not back when Betty and Angel came in together, to find the blank slate and Godfrey's high chair pushed up to the table, but no one in the room. They called his name about the garden and paddock, and just as Betty was beginning to get into a panic and to declare it was all her fault, he appeared, coming back slowly across the field towards the wicket gate. The two aunts met him, Angel looking grieved and Betty indignant.

'Godfrey, this is very naughty,' began Angel, gravely.

'I don't see that you can have any heart at all,' said Betty, 'because it's quite plain you want to break both ours. Perhaps when we are both in our graves, with stones over us like Miss Jane's—only we couldn't afford near such large ones—you'll feel something pricking you.'

'I know I shall,' said her nephew promptly, 'because then Penny would pin my collar, and she always sticks the point of the pin inside.'

'Godfrey,' said Angel gravely, 'this isn't a thing to laugh at. Where have you been?'

'To Farmer White's pond to have a naval battle,' said Godfrey frankly.

'You must never go to that pond alone; it is deep in the middle and very dangerous, and you have disobeyed Aunt Betty. Next time you do it, I—I shall be obliged to whip you.'

Angel's voice faltered, and she turned a little pale as she spoke. In those days most little boys were whipped for disobedience, and Angel had always had a dreadful feeling that she might have to do it some day. There was no one else whose business it was to punish Godfrey, and so she knew that the duty would have to be done by herself, and the very thought made her feel quite cold and shaky.

Godfrey looked straight into her eyes.

'Yes, Aunt Angel,' he said. Then he suddenly took hold of her hand and stroked it.

'I didn't want to crack your heart, and Aunt Betty's,' he said. 'Please don't get thin; I'm sorry I had the battle. I'll go home now, and write all about the cover-up-candle-bell.'

For the next few days there was no fault to find with the way Godfrey's lessons were learnt, and he watched for every chance of pleasing Angelica, as if he were really afraid of her heart cracking, as Betty had suggested it might. The weather was cold and frosty now, and the two young aunts were much disturbed at the idea of Godfrey's first winter in a northern climate. Angel consulted with Penny and Martha, and stitched away diligently to provide the necessary warm clothes, and he certainly looked much stronger already than when he had first come to Oakfield.

There came a day, a bright, frosty day in December, when both the young ladies were in the kitchen helping Penelope with the mince-meat for Christmas pics, and Godfrey had his sum to do in the parlour by himself. Outside the sun was shining. There had been a little sprinkling of snow the day before and a sharp frost at night, and all the garden was white and sparkling like the ice on a sugared cake, while the bare trees shone like fairy land. Godfrey's eyes would not keep on the grey figures and the black slate. It was his first English winter, you see, and it seemed to him like Aunt Betty's stories of enchantment. And besides, only last night, when they sat together in the window seat and watched the stars coming out keen and clear above the white world, she had told him about Arctic discoverers, and how they sailed away over the grey northern seas till the ice barred their way, and how the bones of many brave men had been left behind in that dread, frozen world. Thinking of those great deeds always made Godfrey's cheeks glow and his heart beat quick, and now he laid down his slate and went and leaned with both elbows on the window ledge and looked out. And looking at what we want and oughtn't to have is a first step which takes us a long way, and the end of it was that Godfrey did as I fear many of us have done before him—left what he ought to do for what he wanted to do; that is to say, he went into the hall, took down his hat and coat, and went out into the frosty garden. He opened the wicket gate into the field, and the first person he saw there was Nancy Rogers, looking like a Christmas card with her red cloak and hood and a basket on her arm, as she came up the steep, snowy path which led across the field to the village.

Godfrey and Nancy were great friends, and she came running directly he called to her.

'Would you like to come for a cruise with me and the *Victory*, Nancy?' he asked.

Nancy knew as well as Godfrey that she had no business to go. Her mother and Patty had their Christmas preparations to make as well, and wanted the eggs she had been to fetch. But, like Godfrey, she put 'want' before 'ought' that afternoon.

'Mother always likes me to do what the young ladies and Master Godfrey want,' she said to herself, and so she turned her face away from home with Godfrey and the *Victory*.

'Please, where is the cruise, Master Godfrey?' she asked, as she trotted along on the frozen snow.

'We are going to sail the *Victory* on Farmer White's pond,' said Godfrey, 'and to watch those white ducks' harbours, for they've got ships building there I know.'

'Oh but, Master Godfrey, please we can't,' exclaimed Nancy; 'the pond's frozen and the ship won't float.'

'Frozen!' exclaimed Godfrey; 'do you mean to say all that water's ice like these puddles?'

Nancy nodded.

'I see it as I come along,' she said. 'Pete says two more nights' frost and we'll be going sliding.'

Godfrey had never been sliding, his thoughts were of Arctic discoverers.

'Very well, Nancy,' he said, 'if we can't watch the harbours we'll find the North-west Passage.'

'Yes, Master Godfrey,' said Nancy readily, and without the least idea what he meant.

'Do you know about the Arctic Circle?' asked Godfrey.

Nancy shook her head doubtfully; at the Oakfield Dame School there was not much taught beyond the 'three R's.'

'Please, is it quite round?' she asked respectfully.

'I don't know about round,' said Godfrey, who didn't quite understand the words himself, 'but I think it is a kind of fairy place. The sea is all ice, they have frost and snow there always.'

'Dear now, how bad for the early potatoes!' remarked Nancy, 'and as for sowing beans, why you might as well leave it alone. I suppose they just keep the cows on turnips year in, year out, poor things!'

'Cows!' said Godfrey scornfully; 'of course there aren't any cows, only Polar bears prowling on the ice. And there are icebergs, great mountains of ice all blue, and they come crashing together and grinding up the ships, like a great giant's teeth, Aunt Betty says. And it's always dark, dark all day for months together.'

'Oh dear!' said Nancy, much awe-struck, 'I shouldn't like to be one of the people that lives there, Master Godfrey.'

'Nobody does live there but the Polar bears, and there's a sort of red light comes in the sky that they can see to prowl by, I suppose, and the stars, I should think they're brighter than even they were last night; weren't they bright last night, Nancy, just about supper time?'

Nancy couldn't say she had noticed; there had been sausages for supper, father had killed a pig.

'But if nobody lives there how do they know about it?' she asked.

'Because brave men have gone there to see,' said Godfrey, with the eager light coming into his eyes. 'Aunt Betty says that country is full of the graves of brave men who have gone up there and died away in the dark and the cold.'

'Poor things!' sighed Nancy. 'I daresay now their friends will have put up nice handsome stones over their graves, won't they?'

'No, there aren't any stones,' said Godfrey; 'Aunt Betty says their deeds are their monuments.'

Nancy looked as if she thought such monuments rather unsatisfactory.

'Father put up a nice stone with a vase a-top of it to his great-uncle,' she remarked, 'and the captain's grandfather he's got two angels crying and a skull at the bottom; it's a nice handsome grave, that is.'

They had reached the pond by this time, a piece of dark water overhung by willows and covered with black ice, which had been broken at one end for the cattle to drink. Godfrey began at once to invent.

'We'll put the *Victory* here,' he said, launching his boat into the dark hole; 'this is the last piece of open water, Nance, and from here we must just take to the ice, you and I, and leave the crew to take care of the ship till we get back. Take your rifle, I see there are Polar bears prowling over there among the icebergs.'

'Where?' asked Nancy, rather alarmed.

'Why there, things with turned-up tails and what you'd p'r'aps take for yellow bills when first you saw them. I should like their fur for Aunt Angel. Now we are going to start to find the North-west Passage. Beyond that place where the Polar bears are no one has ever been, and no one knows what is there.'

'Oh yes, please, Master Godfrey, I do,' exclaimed Nancy, ready as usual with information; 'the pig-sty.'

'Nobody knows that comes with me on the *Victory*', persisted Godfrey firmly, 'or if they do they've got to think they don't know as soon as possible. Now, say good-bye to the crew and come along.'

Nancy did not find it so easy as Godfrey seemed to do to imagine the empty decks of the little *Victory* fully manned, so her good-byes did not take long. But when she found that her captain's intention was to cross the pond on the ice, she hung back.

'It won't bear, Master Godfrey; Pete said it wasn't going to bear to-day.'

'What's bear?' asked Godfrey, with a foot on the ice.

'You can't walk on it, it'll break,' urged Nancy.

'What'll happen if it does?' asked Godfrey, with interest. That dark smooth surface, the first ice he had ever trodden on, had a strange attraction for him.

'You'll be drowned,' said Nancy solemnly; 'Pete knew a man whose brother was drowned through the ice. He'd had a drop too much beer and he got off the path.'

'There isn't any path here and I don't drink beer,' said Godfrey loftily. 'Are you coming?'

'Oh, if you please, Master Godfrey, I think I'd sooner stop with the crew!' faltered Nancy.

'Very well,' said Godfrey calmly; 'if I leave my bones in the Arctic Circle, go home in the *Victory* and take the news to my countrymen in England.'

'Oh, Master Godfrey, do come back!' screamed Nancy, for the ice was really swaying; 'it won't be only your bones, it will be all of you if it breaks.'

'I can't hear you,' said Godfrey, with his back to her; 'you and the crew are miles away, I'm beyond where the foot of anything ever trod except Polar bears. Why, what's that?' and he doubled up his hand and looked through it for a telescope.

'It's the tub they used to use for the pig-wash,' exclaimed Nancy; 'it's frozen into the ice. Oh, Master Godfrey, do come back!'

'Some other discoverer has been here before me,' said Godfrey gravely, without noticing her. 'I see the hulk of a vessel locked in the ice, and unless I am mistaken she flies English colours. I must board her and see whether — —'

A shriek from Nancy and a dreadful rumbling crack cut short his speech, and the next moment Godfrey knew what was meant by ice not bearing. The smooth surface gave way under him, the cold water was round his feet, and in an instant he would have been underneath it altogether but for the tub, to which he clung with all his might. There was a dreadful moment while Nancy screamed at the top of her voice and Godfrey's knees and feet battered the tub in the cold black water, then with the triumphant exclamation, 'I've boarded her,' he tumbled over into it.

Luckily the tub, though old, was fairly water-tight, and bobbed up and down with Godfrey inside it in the big hole which he had made, and though a wide space of cracked ice and dark water lay between him and the shore, he seemed to be safe for the present. As for Nancy, she did the wisest thing she could and rushed down the lane calling for help. She did not have to run far. Almost directly she heard steps on the frosty road, quickened at the sound of her screams, and a gentleman came round the bend of the lane, sending his voice before him as he shouted: 'What's the matter?'

His own eyes told him quicker than Nancy's breathless explanation.

'All right,' he exclaimed, 'he's safe while he keeps still. Don't cry, little woman, and I'll tow him ashore.'

The next minute he had dragged a rail from a broken fence close by and held it out to Godfrey.

'Hold tight,' he said; 'stand in the middle so that you balance your craft. Now then, a long pull and a strong pull,' and in another minute he had dragged the tub through the drifting ice to the bank and was lifting Godfrey out.

'There, young man,' he said as he set him on his feet, 'lucky for you you're safe ashore, for this pond's deep enough to cover half-a-dozen giants of your height. How came you cruising among the ice in a leaky craft, I should like to know?'

'I boarded her because the ice broke,' said Godfrey frankly; 'I didn't know it was going to break.'

'No, I don't suppose you did. Lucky for you that you had her to board, young gentleman. Now then, right about face, and put your best foot foremost, and home as fast as you can before you get cold. Where do you live?'

'At Oakfield,' said Godfrey, picking up the *Victory*.

'At Oakfield, do you? Then we shall have the pleasure of each other's company, for I am going that way. Let's see how fast you can walk.'

Godfrey and Nancy trotted beside him as he strode along the frosty road.

'Now what put it into your head to come and look for frozen-up craft in the pond here?' he asked.

'I didn't,' said Godfrey. 'I came to watch the French ports, and then I found it had turned into the Arctic Circle, so I went after the North-west Passage instead. I wanted to be like one of those brave men.'

'Did you, though? And what particular heroes do you want to imitate?'

'I want to be a brave sailor,' said Godfrey promptly, 'like Lord Nelson, and Admiral Collingwood, and most of all Kiah Parker's Captain Maitland.'

'And why "most of all"? I hope you'll be a braver man and a finer fellow than that, young man.'

Godfrey's head only reached about as high as the gentleman's elbow, but he looked at him with as much scorn as if he had been a head taller.

'You don't understand a bit about it,' he said; 'nobody could be a finer fellow than the captain if he tried all his life long. P'r'aps you don't know about him carrying the little cabin-boy below with the French bullets flying all round; you'd better get Kiah to tell you, and then you'll be sorry you've been so stupid.'

'Oh well, we won't quarrel about such an unimportant person. What house in Oakfield do you live in?'

'At Oakfield Cottage,' said Godfrey, still a little distrustful of a man who called Captain Maitland an unimportant person.

'Oh, I remember going to Oakfield Cottage when I was a little boy. And whom do you live with?'

'With my two maiden aunts,' said Godfrey.

'They're so good!' put in Nancy, who liked to have her word in the conversation.

'I've no doubt they are. Now I haven't got any aunts at all that I know of, married or single. We'd better not tell these good ladies how nearly their nephew was at the bottom of the pond or we shall frighten them out of their wits, I'm afraid.'

'Oh, but I must,' said Godfrey, gravely, 'because they told me not to come, and I did, and Aunt Angel's going to whip me.'

'Ah, well, of course we must tell the truth then, and perhaps if I beg for you I might get her to let you off the whipping.'

Godfrey shook his head.

'Aunt Angel always does what she says,' he remarked.

'Well, she's quite right there,' said his new friend, though to himself he thought,

'Poor little chap, he's small for flogging. I wonder if the old lady's hand is heavy.'

Then he asked aloud,

'What made you come Arctic exploring if you knew the whipping was to follow?'

'I didn't like my sum,' confessed Godfrey, 'and I did want to be like those brave men.'

'Ah,' said the stranger thoughtfully, 'do you know, little chap, you've begun at the wrong end? What do you think makes a brave man?'

'Killing lots of Frenchmen,' said Godfrey promptly.

'Not a bit of it. Now, little maid, what do you say?'

'I think, please sir, that brave men don't mind when Frenchmen kill them, and shoot their legs and their fingers off like Uncle Kiah's.'

'That's nearer the mark, but that's not all. The bravest men are the ones that do what they don't like because it's right, and leave what they do like because it's wrong.'

Godfrey's grave eyes looked up at the gentleman's face as they were used to looking at his Aunt Angel. After a minute he said, slowly,

'Should I have been more like the captain if I'd stayed and done the sum instead of going to be an Arctic discoverer?'

'You'd have been more like a hero, my lad, and you will be another time, I know. This is the way to Oakfield Cottage, isn't it? Do you live there too, little lass?'

'Oh no, sir,' said Nancy; 'we live at the Place, sir, and take care of it for the captain.'

'Do you, though! And is it hard work?'

Nancy looked as important as if the welfare of the whole house depended on her efforts.

'Of course one can't help thinking a deal about what he'll say when he comes home,' she said. 'Patty says he'll as like as not be very particular in his ways. Sailors get to be that neat, she says. She always says it if I racket about or if I spill anything or break things.'

'Well, I wouldn't frighten myself before he comes, if I were you,' said the stranger good-naturedly. 'I shouldn't be surprised if he's not so very alarming. These people who look so big from a distance are often small enough when you get them close. Ah, there's the Cottage, I remember it, and somebody coming to the gate to look for you. These are your sisters, I suppose; you didn't tell me you had any sisters.'

'No,' said Godfrey, 'these are my aunts.'

Then he ran straight forward and had hold of Angelica's dress in a moment, looking up straight into her face.

'Aunt Angel,' he began, when Betty stopped him by a scream.

'Godfrey, you're wet! Wherever have you been?'

'I've been in the pond,' said Godfrey's clear voice; 'I mean my legs have. Before that I was on the ice, but it broke, and then there was only water for me to be on. If there hadn't been a tub I should have been at the bottom. Aunt Angel, Aunt Angel dear, don't look like

73

that; your cheeks are quite white—oh, is your heart cracking? I've come for you to whip me; please whip me quick. I wanted to be brave, and I've begun at the wrong end.'

'Oh, Godfrey, how could you, how could you?' faltered Betty.

'It wasn't at all difficult, Aunt Betty,' said Godfrey earnestly; 'p'r'aps that was why it wasn't brave.'

'I beg your pardon,' said the stranger, who had been standing by unnoticed, 'but, if I might suggest, I would get this young gentleman's wet things off, and I'm sure he'll be none the worse, and will be wiser another time.'

Angel pulled herself together and made a grave curtsey.

'Thank you, sir, for your kindness in bringing our nephew home. He shall come indoors and get dry at once. Godfrey, come with me,' and she curtsied again and led Godfrey into the house. Betty was following when Nancy rushed up to her and whispered eagerly:

'Please Miss Bet—Miss Elizabeth, the gentleman got Master Godfrey safe out of the tub. I don't know what we should ha' done if it hadn't ha' been for him.'

'I'll run and thank him again,' said Betty impulsively; 'what's his name, Nance?'

'I don't know, miss; I never saw him before.'

think p'r'aps I ought to ask him in,' said Betty, and she followed the stranger down the lane. He turned at the sound of her steps and took off his hat.

'I'm afraid you think us very rude, sir,' she said, with a pretty blush, 'but we were—we were thinking very much about our nephew, you see; he has no one but us to think for him. We are very much obliged indeed to you, my sister and I. Will you—will you come in and have a glass of elder wine, if you have far to go in the cold?'

'Thank you very much,' said the stranger heartily. 'I shall hope to avail myself of your kind hospitality another day, for I am staying a short time in Oakfield, and shall hope to see more of your nephew, who seems to me a very fine little fellow. I must ask my friend here to show me the shortest cut to Oakfield Place,' and he looked at the astonished Nancy with a sly smile. 'My name is Maitland, Captain Maitland of the *Mermaid*. Come along, little woman, and make a clean breast of the Arctic expedition,' and he took off his hat again, gave his hand to Nancy, who could do nothing but stare at him with her mouth and eyes wide open, and went off down the road. It must be confessed that Betty, though she was thirteen years old and an aunt, stared very hard after him too, and stood by the garden gate in the darkening winter afternoon looking with all her eyes down the lane, as if one of the heroes of her history books had suddenly come to life. Then she turned round and rushed back to the house and half-way up the stairs, burning to tell her news. But there she stopped short suddenly, and after a minute sat down on the stairs and dropped her chin in her hands. There she sat without moving until the door of Godfrey's room opened and Angelica came out. The two sisters sprang to meet each other.

'Oh, Angel!' burst out Betty.

'Oh, Betty, I've done it!' and Angel sank down on the stairs, and hid her face on her sister's shoulder.

'Have you whipped him?' asked Betty.

'Yes, I said I would, and I had to; you know what Martha said—he must be able to depend on what we said. I whipped him and put him to bed.'

'Poor Angel, poor dear, how your hands are shaking. You couldn't have hit him very hard.'

'I don't know; it seemed to me as if I did, and he is so little.'

'Did he cry?' asked Betty.

'Oh no, but he's so brave he wouldn't, not even if I really hurt him dreadfully.'

The idea of slender, gentle Angelica doing bodily violence to any one would have been amusing if the sisters had not been too serious to see it.

'Penny met us on the stairs,' Angel went on, 'and she wanted to pet him, and I wouldn't let her. I think she thought me very cruel, and if she knew I'd whipped him——'

'Well, we ar'n't bringing up Godfrey to please Penny,' said Betty decidedly, 'and really and truly, Angel dear, I expect you hurt yourself more than you did him. Come down into the parlour, your fingers are as cold as ice. I've got something to tell you, too.'

She put her arm round her sister's waist, and drew her downstairs, telling the remarkable news about the strange gentleman as they went. Angel could not but be interested.

'Captain Maitland,' she said, 'was it really? Do you know I hardly saw him, I only had a sort of idea that there was a gentleman there. I hope I was not very rude. I ought to have said something more to him.'

'But I did, Angel, so it doesn't matter. I offered him elder wine—that was all right, wasn't it? But I was so glad when he said no, for you know that little last piece of cake is getting stale, and we don't bake till to-morrow, and Penny might have been cross about getting the wine hot with all the mince-meat about.'

'Perhaps it was as well,' said Angelica rather abstractedly. 'How odd it should have been Captain Maitland, Godfrey's hero, that brought him home! Did Godfrey know who he was?'

'I don't think so; I'm sure Nancy didn't. I'm not sure whether he's quite like what I expected, Angel.'

Angel scarcely answered, there was not much room for any one except Godfrey in her thoughts at that moment. Penelope came in presently with a log for the fire, and an air of severe disapproval about her, and asked stiffly whether the poor dear young gentleman upstairs were to have any supper or not. Angel ordered bread-and-milk very quietly, but in such a way that Penny went out of the room with no more than a half-suppressed snort.

'She hates me,' sighed Angel sorrowfully; 'I wonder if Godfrey does.'

'He isn't such a stupid,' said Betty stoutly; and they sat together silent in the twilight, missing the little figure that always squeezed up between them during that idle half-hour—''twixt the gloaming and the mirk.' At last Angel stood up and said, almost appealingly:

'Betty, don't you think I might go to him now?'

'Angel dear, I've been biting my tongue for ever so long to keep from saying it. I'm quite sure you might.'

Angel waited for no more. She was upstairs directly and pausing at Godfrey's door. How would he meet her? Would he be sulky? Would he refuse to speak to her? She hesitated with her fingers on the handle. Then she heard Godfrey's voice inside. He seemed to be saying his lessons.

'England is an island; an island is a piece of land, and I'm not going to say what it is surrounded by, but I know. France is a country, and the capital of it is Paris, and I'm not going to say what there is between France and England, nor what there are sailing about there, but I know.'

'Godfrey,' said Angelica softly in the doorway.

'Aunt Angel!' and a pair of arms were stretched out in the dusk, and Angel's head drawn down until her face was close to Godfrey's own.

'Aunt Angel, Aunt Angel dear, I can't see you in the dark, but I'm feeling your cheeks to see if they are thin. Do you feel at all as if your heart was cracking? Promise me you and Aunt Betty won't be like that Aunt Jane.'

'We shall both be very happy, Godfrey, if you are sorry for being naughty, not only for vexing us,' said Angel with a deep breath of relief.

'I am,' said Godfrey eagerly; 'I won't again. I've begun directly beginning at the right end. Did you hear me beginning at the right end, Aunt Angel?'

'The right end of what, dear?'

'Of being a brave man. That gentleman said it was doing what you didn't like because it was right, and leaving the nice things because they were wrong. So I'm saying my geography, and leaving out all the parts about ships. Do you think he knows, Aunt Angel? I think he is a good man, only rather stupid.'

'What makes you think he's stupid, Godfrey?'

'Because he didn't seem to think that Kiah's captain was a very, very great man. But I daresay he was only ignorant, and Aunt Betty says we should never be hard on ignorance.'

Angel smiled in the dark.

'I can tell you why he said that, Godfrey,' she said. 'Do you know, that gentleman is Captain Maitland himself?'

Godfrey sat upright, and Angel could feel rather than see his wide eyes fixed upon her.

'Him! That man that got me out of the tub! he whispered, in an almost awe-struck voice; 'is that Kiah's captain? And I never knew.'

'You'll see him again,' Angel said, tucking him up fondly; 'he is coming to see us, he told Aunt Betty so.'

Godfrey was silent for fully a minute. Then he said, doubtfully:

'But why did he say that? Because he must know how brave he is.'

'I don't think that really brave, good people ever think much of themselves,' said Angel thoughtfully.

'Why don't they?'

'I think,' said Angelica, turning over the thought in her slow deliberate way, 'I think, Godfrey, it is because they expect more of themselves. It is like going up a mountain, the higher you get the further you see, and you see heights above you and don't feel as if you had got very far. When people begin to be a little brave and good they see better what real courage and goodness mean, and they aren't satisfied with themselves.'

Godfrey had drawn her face down on to the pillow beside him.

'I suppose he knows a great deal about being brave,' he said. 'Do you think he does what he doesn't like when it's right?'

'Yes, Godfrey dear, I expect he does.'

'So do you, don't you? I know you didn't like whipping me; I know what your face is like when things hurt you. Dear little Aunt Angel, you sha'n't make that face any more for me; you're beginning at the right end of being brave, I suppose. I didn't know before you could be brave, but I thought it was all killing Frenchmen. Tell me something: do women have to do that, what you said about leaving the world better?'

'Oh yes, Godfrey,' whispered Angel. It was easy to talk, she felt, here in the dusk, with the soft cheek pressed against hers. 'Even if they can't do any great work themselves, perhaps they can help those who do.'

'Like you and Aunt Betty and me. I'm your little oak-tree, like godpapa Godfrey's, and you planted me and you look after me. And you'd like me to come up brave and be a great captain and win a battle one day. Would you mind if the Frenchies shot my leg off, like Kiah's?'

'I should have to try to be proud, Godfrey; it would be very hard.'

'Then you'd be brave again, wouldn't you—braver than me, because I don't know that I should mind if I was as nice as Kiah? And p'r'aps the King would want me to have a medal, and I should say, "No, please, not for me, your Majesty"; and he'd say, "Who for, then?" and I should say, "For my maiden aunts."'

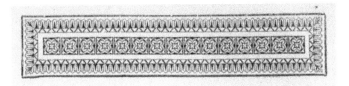

CHAPTER VI

CHRISTMAS AT OAKFIELD

'Round the world and home again,
That's the sailor's way.' —WILLIAM ALLINGHAM

aptain Maitland did call at the cottage, as he had said, the very day after Godfrey's adventure. Angel and Betty felt a little alarmed, for they never had any visitors except the vicar of the parish of which Oakfield was an outlying hamlet. They sat up rather straight on the company chairs in the parlour, and Penelope, who had kept the visitor waiting at the door while she put on her best cap, brought in a bottle of gooseberry wine and a plate of sweet biscuits, for the cake which Angel had hoped would be ready against the time when the captain called was still in the oven. Perhaps it was the disappointment about the cake that upset Penny's ideas, for she never looked where she was going as she came in with the tray, and the consequence was that she stumbled over the round footstool with two wool-work doves sitting in a wreath of roses. It was a dreadful moment, while Penny came staggering forward with the gooseberry wine slipping off the tray, until she went full tilt into the arms of the captain, who had sprung to his feet, and managed very adroitly to catch the tray in one hand and hold up Penny with the other, while the sweet biscuits hailed upon him like bullets. Poor Penny turned and ran, with her cap over one ear, too much abashed even to see what damage was done, and Betty felt that if only the floor would open under her it would be a comfort. Only for half a moment. Then the captain turned round and said, with a most comical expression:

'I can't drink this whole bottle by myself. May I pour you out a glass?'

Betty could do nothing but burst out laughing, and Angel, in spite of her dismay, joined in, and as to Captain Maitland, he laughed out more heartily than any of them, and from that moment there was no more stiffness between them. The captain, though he seemed quite old to Godfrey, and indeed to his aunts too, was not thirty, for he had attained his promotion rapidly for courage and coolness in an encounter off the French coast. He had the frank cheery manners of a sailor too, so that it was not difficult to feel at home with him; besides, as Betty said afterwards, where was the use of pretending they didn't remember that he had had Penny in his arms, and that he had been on his knees under the table picking up the sweet biscuits?

He would be at home for about a fortnight, he said; he had not been to Oakfield for nearly seven years, not since his mother's death; and Angel thought the bright sunburnt face looked a little wistful, and felt sorry for him having no one to welcome him. But he smiled again directly as he said how glad he was to find the place so little changed; and then he asked if he might see the garden, he remembered being brought there when he was a very little boy; did the clove pinks still grow in the border under the yew hedge? So they all went out together, and the captain had forgotten nothing and greeted Miss Jane as an old friend; there had been a ship in the squadron off the Spanish coast, he said, whose figurehead always reminded him of her. And he remembered the view from the paddock, and missed the big elm that had been blown down two winters ago, and said what a good thing it was the storm had spared Sir Godfrey's tree; it would be a misfortune indeed if anything happened to that, but it seemed all right at present, as stout a heart of oak as the Admiral's flag-ship. And he heard that Cousin Crayshaw was coming down for Christmas, and said he remembered him and should do himself the honour of calling upon him. And then they all walked with him to the end of the lane.

'Do you know,' Betty said as they turned, back, 'I keep on forgetting that he is Kiah's captain, and yet I like to think he is.'

Angel and Godfrey felt much the same. It did seem so impossible that this cheery, simple man, who had laughed over the gooseberry wine, and been so interested in the garden, could be the hero who would perhaps be in the history books of the future. Why, they had been talking the whole time, telling him about the great gale which had blown the elm down, when he knew what a storm at sea was like, with waves mountains high, and mighty ships and brave men swallowed up among them, and he had asked about the bees and the best way of layering pinks as if he really cared to know. Could he have room in his thoughts for such simple things when strife and danger and bloodshed and the life-and-death struggle of nations were familiar to him?

As Betty said, they found it hard to believe, and yet it was very nice to think of, and seemed to mean that being a hero need not take one quite away from everything that other people loved and cared about, just as the good Admiral Collingwood noted on the eve of a great sea-fight that it was his little Sarah's birthday, and remarked while the French were pouring their broadside into his ship that his wife would be just going to church. And gentle Angel said to herself that perhaps after all, when Godfrey was a great man, he might be her Godfrey still if he could manage to copy Captain Maitland. And, meanwhile, she felt very glad and thankful on her boy's account for the captain's coming; for here at last, she said to herself, was what she had wanted so long, some one whom he could look up to and admire and try to copy. What a happy thing it was that he should have learnt from his first hero that lesson that the beginning of victory is the conquest of self.

Cousin Crayshaw was to arrive two days before Christmas, and Godfrey and his aunts had been busy decorating the cottage with holly for the occasion. Cousin Crayshaw was not a particularly interesting visitor certainly, but Betty, from the top of the stepladder, told Godfrey, with all the more emphasis because she didn't quite feel it herself, that they ought to be very thankful they had somebody to welcome.

Martha said that welcoming kept people's hearts warm. The two aunts and the nephew all had their own delightful Christmas secrets, and there was much whispering and great excitement and solemn taking of pennies out of Godfrey's money-box when Pete went to the county town with some hay. It was a very serious matter, for of course he could not consult the aunts, and he felt very important when he ran down to meet Pete, and waited at the end of the lane, jingling the pennies and listening to the sound of approaching cart-wheels. Peter saw the little figure waiting, and jumped down at once.

'Anything I can do in town for you, Master Godfrey?' he asked.

'Yes,' said Godfrey, very seriously, 'I am going to give you some money to spend, Pete, to spend on presents. I want two very beautiful presents for two ladies, and a little one that would suit an old nurse.'

'Certainly, sir,' said Pete gravely.

Godfrey jingled his pennies thoughtfully.

'There's a good deal of money,' he remarked. 'Perhaps there might be some over.'

'Very true, sir,' said Pete with much seriousness. Godfrey considered again. Then that happy Christmas feeling which makes our hearts widen to all the world got the best of it:

'If there should be any over, Pete,' he said, 'I should like you to choose another present.'

'I shall be proud to do my best, sir. Would the present be for a lady or a gentleman, sir?'

'For a gentleman, Pete. A gentleman not very young and not at all handsome, that doesn't care much about nice things or pretty things, so it mustn't be an ornament; and that only reads the paper, so it mustn't be a story-book; and that doesn't like any games, so it mustn't be anything to play with. Do you think you could do that, Pete?'

'I'd try, Master Godfrey. It 'd be a useful thing, now, the gentleman would fancy?'

'Yes, certainly useful,' said Godfrey decidedly; 'and rather cheerful too, if you could manage it, for Cousin Cray—I mean the gentleman—isn't a very cheerful gentleman, and I thought perhaps a present might make him a little more cheerful for Christmas.'

'And I'm to spend all this money, Master Godfrey?'

'Yes, all,' said Godfrey generously, pouring his pennies into Pete's hand; 'you're not to bring back one.'

'I do like giving presents,' he went on, as Pete counted the money and put it in his big leathern purse. 'If I had a lot more money I know what I'd do. I'd tell you to choose a present for a gentleman that is one of the very bravest, best people in the world, a gentleman that likes ships and fighting and gardens and flowers, and is always kind to every one except people he ought to kill; but I should think it would take nearly a hundred pounds to buy a present that would be good enough for him. Good-bye, Pete; I shall try and run round to the Place before lessons to-morrow to see what you've got.'

But Godfrey had not to wait till next morning, for just before his bed-time Penny came to the parlour door to say that Peter was in the kitchen and asking for the young master.

'It's business,' said Godfrey with an air of great importance—Betty always called any talk 'business' that Godfrey was not meant to hear. 'Please, Aunt Angel, let Penny stop here while Pete and I are talking in the kitchen.'

Pete was standing by the back door, with a sprinkling of snow on his hat and shoulders, and as Godfrey appeared he brought out from some safe pocket various parcels very tightly tied up, which, when they were undone, displayed a china cup with

'Remember me
  When this you see'

on it in gold letters, two china lambs lying under a tree, and a needle-book with a picture of Queen Charlotte outside. Godfrey was lost in admiration. They were perfect, they were just the very things. The lambs would stand on Aunt Betty's table and the cup would hold Aunt Angel's tea, and the needle-book would suit Penny exactly. 'And was there any more, Pete?' he asked. 'There couldn't have been, surely.'

Pete, for answer, produced another parcel from the depths of his pocket, and exhibited a wooden wafer-box, painted bright red, and with a picture of Mr. Pitt on the lid. Pete watched with the deepest interest while Godfrey opened it.

'You see, Master Godfrey,' he said, 'I was a-thinking the gentleman would be bound to do a deal of writing; and as you said he was partial to newspapers, seemed to me Mr. Pitt would come kind o' natural to him seeing they seem to be mostly about him; and the red colour looks sort o' cheerful and might liven the gentleman up. Hoping it meets your fancy, Master Godfrey.'

'I think it's beautiful,' said Godfrey earnestly; 'you are a very clever person, Pete. Do you mean to say you got it all for that money?'

The smile on Pete's face broadened out, till it reached nearly from ear to ear.

'Well, sir,' he said, 'fact is, for its size and being such a good article, it was wonderful cheap, and there was some money out when I paid for it. And you being so particular about my not bringing a penny home, seemed to me I'd risk bringing this little thing here, in case it might come in handy for what you were talking about.'

So saying, Pete brought out another parcel, and out of the paper came a second box, coloured dark blue this time, and adorned with a picture of a ship in full sail, surrounded by a wreath of convolvulus.

'You see, Master Godfrey,' explained Pete, 'it seemed to me, with you saying the gentleman had a fancy for ships and flowers, and the colour being blue, which stands for sailors, it did seem the sort o' thing you were just a-wishing for.'

'But, Pete,' said Godfrey, as if hardly daring to believe in so grand an idea, 'do you think that sort of gentleman would be likely to be using wafers?'

'Bound to, sir,' said Pete promptly; 'you see, he'd be writing to the Admiral about all the fine things him and his ship was doing, and besides he'd be writing home to folks he was fond of, folks that thought about him, and—and gave him presents and such like.'

'Oh no, Pete, no,' said Godfrey, almost breathless, 'he wouldn't be writing to those sort of people. But really, Pete, I do think the box is very, very beautiful; and do you think—do you think he would be offended if I gave it to him?'

'I'll warrant he'd be as pleased as you like, Master Godfrey,' said Pete heartily; 'he's not the sort to take offence, isn't the captain. Why, bless you, Nancy brought him in a few berries out o' the hedges on Sunday and he made such a work with them as you never saw.' Pete had dropped the little fiction about the gentleman in his interest, and Godfrey did not object.

'I'm very, very much obliged to you, Pete,' he said earnestly; 'I'm as happy as ever I can be. Good-night, dear Pete, and thank you very, very much.'

And so came Christmas, the children's festival, touching home life and child life with its great majesty and beauty. Can any one dare to despise simple things and simple souls when all Christendom comes adoring to a poor cradle and angels stoop to sing carols to shepherd folk? Some such thoughts came into Angelica Wyndham's mind when Nancy ran over on Christmas Eve, very eager and excited, with the captain's compliments, and would Mr. Crayshaw and the young ladies and Master Godfrey dine with him next day; and, please, she did hope they would come, for they were all going to have snap-dragon, and the captain had sent her out with such a lot of money to buy the raisins. And Angel wondered whether after all it was not surprising but right and natural that the captain should care for such things. Wasn't it the Christmas lesson that the great and the simple lie close together, and that the men who are foremost in the midst of death and danger have room in their hearts for children and flowers and home joys and Christmas games as well? And then Cousin Crayshaw had said he would go, and had declared he had a great respect for Captain Maitland. Altogether, it was the happiest Christmas that the sisters had ever spent at Oakfield. And I think there must have been some magic about that cheerful wafer-box with the picture of Mr. Pitt. Mr. Crayshaw found it on his plate on Christmas morning, with an inscription upon it which had been composed by Pete, but written in Godfrey's own firm round hand, and with spelling which was also quite Godfrey's own—'To my deer and respekted cuzon.' And something about the box or the inscription—or was it just a Christmas thought which they put into his head?—made Mr. Crayshaw turn away to the window as if to admire the striking likeness of Mr. Pitt, and then take off his spectacles and rub them and put them on again; and then he did what he had never done before, came round to Godfrey's chair, and put his hands on the little boy's shoulders and kissed his forehead. They walked to church along the ringing frosty road, with the wide white common spreading away on each side like the snow-fields of Godfrey's Arctic stories. And at the churchyard gate they paused, because there were two figures going slowly up the path before them, Captain Maitland, walking erect and steady, with old Kiah Parker on his arm.

'Easy now, easy now, Kiah,' he was saying, 'you'll have me on my nose if you go that pace, man; you and I are more at home on deck than on slippery ground; don't send me sprawling at the very church door, my hearty.'

And as for Kiah, he looked prouder than the Admiral of the Fleet.

After church, however, he hobbled on ahead with Peter and Nancy, while the captain stayed to speak to the party from the cottage. He had had the most beautiful Christmas present, he said, just the very one thing he couldn't have done without any longer. And somebody must have chosen it just to suit him, for it was a real bit of the old blue, and as for the ship, why the *Mermaid* might have sat for the portrait.

'Just the thing for a present to a sailor from a sailor that is to be,' he said; and Godfrey looked as if he had nothing else in the world to wish for.

'Are you going to let me have the little lad one day, sir?' the captain said to Mr. Crayshaw, when Godfrey had walked on in front between his two aunts.

'You do him very great honour, sir,' said the lawyer. 'I have not thought much at present about the boy's future career. He has been a difficulty, Captain Maitland, something of a difficulty. I was afraid that his unfortunate surroundings during his early childhood had had a very bad effect upon his character; but he is much improved, very much improved indeed. You think something may be made of him?'

'I think he is the sort of stuff that heroes are made of,' said the captain thoughtfully, 'and he has such influence about him now as makes heroes.'

Mr. Crayshaw glanced at the three in front of him and coughed in an embarrassed way.

'Angelica is—is a very good girl,' he said; 'indeed they are both very good girls, very good girls. I had my doubts as to the desirability of leaving Godfrey under their charge, but I feel satisfied now that at present I could hardly do better for him.'

'I think he is having such training as will bless his whole life,' said Captain Maitland gravely, and Mr. Crayshaw did not contradict him. Perhaps a thought came over him that if he had had a gentle Angelica and a bright, loving Betty beside him when he was young, his life might have been a better and a more beautiful thing.

An invitation to dinner was such a rare thing at Oakfield that there was a good deal of excitement about getting ready for it. Penny and Angel and Betty all brushed Godfrey's hair in turn, until he was thankful to escape and leave his aunts to get dressed on their own account. But he very soon came rushing upstairs again two steps at a time, and asked eagerly at their door if he might come in.

'Aunt Angel, Aunt Betty, look!' he exclaimed as he burst into the room, 'presents, from Cousin Crayshaw. Oh, do look! — A seal, a real proper seal that belonged to grandpapa, with words on, that makes a mark when you hold it down on your hand hard. And this box has got things in for you; he said so. He was so funny, and he said it so fast I didn't hear it all; but he said I was to give it to you, Aunt Angel, because it was yours really, and perhaps it would help you to remember some things that were past and to forget some others. What did he mean? Only open it, do open it!'

So Angel opened the box, with Betty looking over her shoulder and peering between her falling curls, and Penny peeping over her. And it was Penny who was the first to exclaim, while she hugged both her young ladies in her delight:

'Oh, bless you, my dears, they're your dear mamma's jewels! Dear, dear! and don't I know 'em if any one does, me that put them on her times enough.'

'Mamma's things! Oh, Angel!' said Betty in hushed tones, touching the trinkets with reverent fingers. Angelica had put her hands before her eyes. A great rush of memory was sweeping over her, for it is the little things that take hold of our minds when we are children, and the sight of them in after years brings the big things in their train. And those pearls used to be twisted among the sunny curls of the head that had bent over her little bed on long ago evenings, and the ruby ring had sparkled on the hand that used to clasp her baby fingers. And that miniature with its gold setting? Did not mamma wear it on a gold chain out of sight? Had not Betty's little restless fingers pulled it out one day, and had not Angel wondered as her mother kissed it with dewy eyes and put it back? Betty was holding it to the light.

'Why, Angel,' she exclaimed wonderingly, 'it's Godfrey.'

And Penny, with her apron to her eyes, explained,

'No, no, my dear, it's his poor dear papa, that's who it is.'

'My papa!' ejaculated Godfrey, with round eyes, 'why, Penny, it's a little boy.'

'And so he was a little boy,' sobbed Penny, 'and the dearest, beautifullest little boy ever I saw or anybody saw, and his dear mamma had his picture done the day he was eight years old, and she wore it till she died, bless her heart.'

Angel bent her head and kissed the laughing face as she had seen her mother kiss it.

'And Cousin Crayshaw sent it to us,' said Betty thoughtfully; 'now I know what he meant about remembering and forgetting.'

'I don't,' said Godfrey, 'but I want Aunt Angel to hang papa's picture round her neck.'

'Yes, yes, Angel, you must,' said Betty eagerly, clasping the chain about her sister's throat; 'you talked to him—you remember—and I don't really, though I'm sure I feel a kind of something as if I should know him.'

'Then you must wear mamma's pearls, Betty dear, you must indeed.'

'No, indeed, I mustn't, because you are going to. Yes, you are, Angel, don't say a word—you are going to wear them in your hair like she used to. Penny, please put up Angel's hair like mamma's picture. I am going to have this dear, dear brooch, with all the twisted bits of gold and the little tiny diamonds; fancy me in diamonds! You ought to have them really, but I know you like the others best.'

And so, a few minutes later, when Angel met Cousin Crayshaw on the stairs, he quite started at the sight of her, with the gold chain round her neck and the pearls among her dark curls.

'You have given us the most beautiful Christmas present in the world, Cousin Crayshaw,' she said, holding out her hands to him. And Mr. Crayshaw, with a sudden impulse, kissed her forehead as he had kissed Godfrey's.

'They were yours already, not mine, my dear,' he said, and then he added:

'You are very like your mother, Angelica, very like indeed.'

I don't think there could have been a merrier party than that Christmas dinner party at Oakfield Place.

Captain Maitland held the same opinion as a wise man who once said that 'it is good to be children sometimes, and never better than at Christmas time, when its mighty Founder was a child Himself.' And the captain had the power of not only being quite childishly happy himself, but of making those about him feel the same. The room was all bright with holly, and when pretty Patty had brought in the Christmas goose, and the captain had handed Angelica with courtly politeness to her place on his right hand, he set himself to keep the whole party laughing, and succeeded very well. For he told stories about Christmases at sea, and days when he was a boy at Oakfield Place, and got into scrapes and out again like other boys who had not grown up into heroes. And then he positively asked Mr. Crayshaw if he hadn't some stories of scrapes to tell, now that they were all making confessions. And before Betty's eyes had got back to their natural size, after her amazement at the idea of Cousin Crayshaw in a scrape, that gentleman was answering, with a sort of little cackle which really was almost a laugh, that he did remember once being out after time on a half-holiday, and finding the school-gate shut and climbing over it, and that his coat caught on the top and he hung there till it tore. And at the thought of Cousin Crayshaw hanging on a nail, Betty at any rate hid her face and laughed till she cried, and I believe Angel wasn't far behind her, and, most wonderful of all, Cousin Crayshaw didn't mind a bit. And when dinner was over, and they had drunk to 'Present Company' and 'Absent Friends,' and Mr. Crayshaw had proposed 'The Navy' in quite a fine speech, and Captain Maitland had proposed 'The Law' in a still finer one, then Patty came in with a twinkle in her eyes and moved away the table and pushed the chairs against the walls. And then the captain remarked that it was a cold night, and wouldn't it be a good thing if they were to warm their feet a little? And the next minute there was the sound of Kiah's wooden leg in the passage, and there he was with his fiddle, and the Rogers, all in their Sunday clothes, just behind him. And Patty ran to put down a line of mats, because wooden legs were not good for polished floors. And the captain made Angel such a bow, as if she had been Queen Charlotte herself, and hoped she would put up with an awkward old sailor for a partner, and he was sure Pete would show them the way with Miss Betty. And Godfrey did his very best to copy the captain as he gave his hand to Nancy. And then happened the most wonderful thing that ever had happened in Oakfield, for as Kiah struck up 'Off she goes!' Mr. Crayshaw suddenly went up to fair-haired Patty, who hardly knew where to look, and told her he had not danced for twenty years, but Christmas seemed the time for a frolic, and he would ask her to help him.

Then, when even Nancy and Godfrey were breathless, there came in one of Martha's best cakes and a big plate full of oranges. And the captain called upon Kiah for a song, which Kiah sang readily enough, and played for himself, too, on the fiddle, with the music a good way behind the words. And then they all joined in the chorus of 'Hearts of Oak,' and after that Angel's sweet voice started 'God rest you, merry gentlemen.' And then out with the lights and in with the blazing dish of snap-dragon! How valiant Godfrey was in pulling out plums for every one; how very, very nearly Betty set her lace ruffles on fire; what queer shadows the flickering light threw on the wall, and how strange the eager faces looked when the captain threw a handful of salt on the fire and the flame burnt blue, while Nancy got half frightened and hid behind Patty's skirts! But at last all the raisins had been pulled out and the fire was dying, and positively there was the clock striking ten! What a time of night for Godfrey and Nancy to be out of bed! But, as the captain said, who looks at the clock at Christmas time? So Martha and her daughters curtsied themselves out of the room, and Mr. Crayshaw stood at the door talking quite cheerily with old Kiah, while Betty kept Pete back a minute to ask about her linnet, which was ill—Pete knew so much about birds.

Godfrey had climbed into the window seat, and was peeping between the curtains to see if it looked like another frost.

'Look at the stars, Aunt Angel dear, aren't they bright? Is the Wise Men's Star there still, do you suppose? That's the Plough, isn't it? If one was up in the Plough could one see Oakfield, do you think?'

'I used to like to think one could,' said the captain, who had come up behind them. 'Many's the time, when I was a little bit of a middy, I used to watch the stars and feel quite friendly to them because they could see home. And the Plough, when I could see it, was a real old friend, I knew the look of it so well from this window.'

'I shall do that when I'm a middy,' said Godfrey gravely, 'and I shall think of them seeing my aunts and Oakfield, and they'll think of them seeing me.'

'So you've quite made up your mind to be a middy?' said the captain, with a hand on Godfrey's shoulder.

'Quite,' said the little boy earnestly; 'Aunt Angel says everybody must be useful, like you and Kiah, and she's teaching me to be. I'm like her's and Aunt Betty's little oak-tree, and they hope I shall grow up a very brave sailor. But she's really braver than me, for she says it will be very hard for her not to mind when the Frenchies shoot my leg off, and I don't think I shall mind much.'

Angel's cheeks were crimson at hearing her own words repeated. She looked so very sweet and womanly as she sat there in the window.

They had not lighted the candles again, and only the flickering fire-light played about her, touching her white dress and the curly locks, knotted up high behind her head, with the gleaming pearls among them.

The captain stroked Godfrey's hair.

'Ay, little man,' he said, 'the bravest hearts are the ones we leave at home; and more shame to us that we're not finer fellows when they take so much thought for us.'

Just then Betty called Godfrey, and he ran to bid Pete good-night. The captain stood looking after him.

'His Majesty's navy will be the richer for that lad one day, Miss Angelica,' he said.

Angel flushed with pleasure.

'I do hope so,' she said simply; 'Betty and I are almost afraid sometimes when we think what we want him to be, and that there is only us to teach him and fit him for it.'

'I don't think you need be afraid,' said Captain Maitland quietly; 'the navy is a rough school, Miss Angelica, but so is the world all over, I fancy, and I've known plenty of men who've lived and died on board as pure and simple as if they'd never left home. And they were mostly men who'd such a home life as your little lad to stick by them and keep them straight. Never mind about special training, just give him something to steer by, and trust me he won't go far wrong.'

CHAPTER VII

HERO AND HEROINES

'For though she meant to be brave and good,
    When he played a hero's part,
Yet often the thought of the leg of wood
    Hung heavy on her heart.' — A.

ell, Christmas time, like all good things, had to come to an end, and so did the captain's stay at Oakfield. The village seemed very dull for a while after he went. Nancy cried bitterly when she said good-bye to him, and indeed so did Patty, and I fancy Betty shed a few tears in Miss Jane's arbour, she ran away there in such a hurry after watching the captain start, and came back with such red rings round her eyes. Good-bye is a hard word at any time, and harder still in war time, when it is overshadowed by that unspoken dread lest no future greeting should come in which the parting may be forgotten. As for Godfrey, when the captain was gone he went over to the Place and sat down in the kitchen by the side of Kiah. Kiah would miss the captain more than any one, but the worst part of the going to him was that he was not going too.

'You and me, young master,' he said to Godfrey, as the child sat on a low stool looking up at him, 'our orders is to bide in port. Only you're fitting for a cruise, you see, sir, and I'm just a hulk that'll never be seaworthy again. It don't become us to be asking questions about our orders, we'd better just get to work and do what we can, so I'll be off and chop a bit of firewood for Martha.'

'And I'll go home and learn my spelling,' said Godfrey.

And, indeed, he was back in the parlour and at work before Betty came to look for him, on which she gave herself one of her indignant scoldings, telling herself that Godfrey was ten times more fit to be her bachelor uncle than she was to be his maiden aunt.

And so the little household at the cottage went back to the quiet life in which Christmas had made such a pleasant break. Angel and Betty read French and history together, and helped Penny in the kitchen, and taught Godfrey, and walked with him, and mended for him and built castles in the air for him when he was in bed and asleep; and Godfrey learnt his lessons and played with Nancy, and spent all the time he could with Kiah, and in the twilight sat crushed up between his aunts in the great arm-chair and talked about what he would do when he was big and a sailor. Cousin Crayshaw came down every other Saturday and stayed till Monday, and Betty asked herself, as she watched him reading his paper in the evening, whether he could be indeed the same Cousin Crayshaw who had climbed over the school gate, and had danced 'hands across and back again' with Patty for his partner. But, though Cousin Crayshaw did not tell school stories or indulge in country dances at the cottage, still the remembrance of that evening was a link between himself and his young cousins which none of them could forget. The girls did not seem to respect him less because they were less afraid of him and because they ventured to talk about their own pleasures and interests in his presence, and indeed now and then he would ask questions himself, would even call Godfrey to him and want to know about his lessons and how he managed to amuse himself. And as the days got longer the three would coax him into the garden to look at their flowers coming up, and one day Betty boldly offered him an auricula for his button-hole. And though he seemed a little doubtful at first as to whether such an ornament would become a grave and sober person like himself, yet he let her put it in for him, and after that there was never a Sunday that some flower did not appear on his plate at breakfast, placed there by each of the three in turn. One evening, while he was reading the paper, he looked up to see Angel standing by his chair.

'Please, Cousin Crayshaw,' she said, with the colour coming into her cheeks, 'might I read to you for a little while, if you think I could read well enough?'

'It wouldn't interest you, Angelica,' said her cousin in surprise.

'Oh yes, it would,' pleaded Angel, 'especially if—if you would explain about it to us a little. We think, Betty and Godfrey and I, that we know so dreadfully little about the affairs of the country, and every one ought to care about their country, oughtn't they? and we want to understand about the war, because, you see, we must care about our soldiers and sailors, and Captain Maitland is there, you know.'

And so Mr. Crayshaw, with a half-amused smile, let her try, and positively found Betty's eager questions very interesting, and really enjoyed explaining difficulties with Angelica's earnest eyes looking up at him, so that the little household at the cottage became quite politicians, and followed the army and the fleet on the map with the deepest interest. And Pete's prediction was fulfilled, for Captain Maitland actually found time to write Godfrey a most interesting letter, which lived in Godfrey's pocket and slept under his pillow at night, till it tore to pieces in the folds, after which Angel mended it with paste, and it was locked into a box upstairs of which Godfrey kept the key, lest thieves should get into the house and steal it. They were stirring times, those first years of our nineteenth century, when the news from abroad was of fierce struggles by land and sea, when the talk by the fireside and in the village streets was of an invasion that might be, when Englishmen would have to stand shoulder to shoulder, and fight on their own thresholds for country and home. All these things, the battles and the sieges, the plans and counter-plans, the great names of men who helped to change the fate of Europe, we read in our history books.

The shadow of the war, the anxiety about the present and fear about the future, must have hung like a cloud over our country in those years, and yet, notwithstanding, life went on quietly in the homes which the great danger was threatening, and people worked and played and laughed, and cared more on the whole about their own small affairs than about the big affairs of Europe. And so, though those years when England's enemies were watching her across the narrow seas, and wise men were planning and brave men fighting for her liberties, are so interesting in the history books, there is not very much to tell about the good folks at Oakfield. In those days, when no one had begun to think about railways, country people left home very little, and the changes of the seasons, sowing and reaping, hay-time and harvest, made the chief events of their lives; and though it seemed very important to Oakfield, it wouldn't be very interesting to any one else to hear of the wonderful apple crop in the orchard at the Place, or of how the miller's pony strayed away on the common and was lost for two days, or of how Godfrey and Nancy missed their way when out blackberrying, and came home after dark to find the aunts half distracted and Rogers and Pete searching, all over the country.

'The slow, sweet hours that bring us all things good.'

Those words always seem to me to describe the quiet years when nothing particular happens, when we are growing and learning almost without knowing it, getting, as Captain Maitland had said, something to steer by in harder, busier days to come. Godfrey, when he looked back afterwards, couldn't remember any very big events in his Oakfield life—just daily lessons and daily games, stories from Betty, twilight talks with Angel, hours spent by old Kiah's bench at the Place—and yet those 'slow sweet hours,' more than the stirring days afterwards, were to influence his whole life and make a man of him.

How surprised his young aunts would have been if any one had told them on the day when their nephew first came to Oakfield that it would be Angel who would suggest to Cousin Crayshaw that it was time for him to leave them. Mr. Crayshaw found her standing by his chair one Sunday evening when he awoke from a little doze in which he had been indulging after supper.

'Cousin Crayshaw,' she began hesitatingly, 'have you thought lately what a big boy Godfrey is getting?'

'Big? Yes, yes, of course, very big,' said Mr. Crayshaw in surprise. 'What's the matter, Angelica? Why shouldn't he grow? He looks strong enough, I'm sure.'

'Oh, he's as strong as a little pony,' said Angel proudly; 'but, Cousin Crayshaw, don't you think he's getting rather big for us to teach?'

'Is he troublesome?' asked Mr. Crayshaw doubtfully.

'Oh no, no! Only Betty and I think he is getting old enough to be taught by a man.'

'Humph! That means school, I suppose,' said Mr. Crayshaw, 'or could we find him a tutor?'

'I think—at least, don't you think it ought to be school?' said Angel hesitatingly. 'I mean, if he is going to sea, oughtn't he to knock about with other boys a little first?'

Her cousin looked up thoughtfully at her.

'You'll miss him a good deal, won't you, my dear?' he said.

'Oh, it doesn't do to think about that,' said Angelica cheerfully.

'And you know, Cousin Crayshaw,' said Betty from her corner, 'you said when first we had him that we weren't to spoil him.'

'No, no, of course not, of course not,' said Cousin Crayshaw heartily; 'I'll inquire about a school.'

There was a little mischievous twinkle in Betty's eyes as she bent over her book, and when she and Angel were alone that night she threw her arms round her sister and burst out laughing. 'Oh, Angel,

Angel, isn't it funny,' she cried, 'to think of you having to make Cousin Crayshaw send Godfrey to school?'

'I believe he is almost as loth to lose him as we are,' said Angel; 'don't you love him for it?'

'Yes, that I do; and do you remember how you wouldn't let me make Godfrey hate him? Angel dear, I'm just wondering how soon I and Godfrey and Penny and this house altogether would go to rack and ruin without you.'

And so Godfrey went to school.

It certainly was hard work letting him go, and Penny wore the same face all day as she had done when Angel had whipped him for disobedience, and evidently thought everybody very hard-hearted. And the house did seem fearfully empty and silent, especially in the first twilight hour, when Angel and Betty sat together in the big chair where there had always been room for a third.

Cousin Crayshaw arrived quite unexpectedly in the middle of the week, and gave no explanation whatever of his coming, except that he had brought Angelica a new book of poems; and how did he come to know Angel liked poetry, for he never read it himself? And better than the unexpected visit, almost better than the book, which Betty read till a dreadful hour that night, was Mr. Crayshaw's sudden exclamation,

'Dear me, how one does miss that boy!'

He was nearly strangled the next moment by Betty's arms thrown round his neck, and though he said,

'Elizabeth! Dear, dear, don't throttle me,' he did not seem angry.

Godfrey was just the sort of boy to get on well at school, and he was soon popular both with boys and masters. In after years there was a packet, put away among Angelica's more cherished possessions, and ticketed, 'Letters written from school by my nephew Godfrey,' and I think even the famous letter from the captain was not more read and re-read. There was one in particular which, I believe, had some tears dropped over it, though it was never shown to Martha and Penny as some of the others were.

'My dear Aunt Angel,' it ran, 'I have had a fight. The boy I fought was bigger than me. He gave me a black eye, but I gave him two. He said something about you and aunt Betty, but he never will again. Jones, who is the head of the school, says I am a good plucked one. He put some raw meat on my eye for me. I thought you might find it useful to know about it; it is the very best thing when anyone's knocked you about, only be sure you put it on at once. I send a kiss to Aunt Betty and one to Penny, and my love to Martha and Pete and Nancy and Kiah and Cousin Crayshaw.

'Your affectionate nephew,
    'GODFREY WYNDHAM.'

'It's like the champions in the days of chivalry,' said Betty, with shining eyes, 'only instead of a beautiful ladye-love, the darling's been fighting and getting wounded just for his two maiden aunts. Angel, I believe that Jones is a dear boy. I should like to send a little cake for him when we send Godfrey one. Angel, do you—do you think it's our duty to scold Godfrey for fighting?'

'I'm not sure,' said Angel slowly; and then she added, for once as decidedly as her sister, 'but I'm sure I'm not going to.'

I expect a diary of the lives of Angelica and Betty for the next year or two would have run something in this way:

'Godfrey came home. Heard from Godfrey. Godfrey writes that the cricket season has begun. Godfrey brought home a prize. Godfrey went back to school' (this last with a very black mark against it). But such a diary, though it was deeply interesting to the two young aunts themselves, wouldn't make much of a story to those who didn't mark time by Godfrey's holidays, and so we must just take a leap over several of these uneventful years and come suddenly to the day which all the time had stood in Angel's mind as a sort of background to everything else that happened, the day which she had taught herself to think about, and which she prayed every day of her quiet life that she might be strong and brave to meet.

It was an autumn day, misty and still, like that on which Godfrey had first come to Oakfield, and Cousin Crayshaw came down in the middle of the week. It was late afternoon, and Angel was catching the last light from the window on her sewing; and when she raised her head at the sound of wheels, and saw her cousin get out of his chaise, she knew in one moment that the day she had been preparing for had come. She put her work down with very trembling hands, and went down the path to meet Mr. Crayshaw, knowing quite well what he had to say to her while he made little nervous remarks about the weather, until at last he took a paper out of his pocket and gave it her to read, watching her anxiously all the while. The writing seem to grow dim and uncertain before Angel's eyes, but she knew what it was—the order for Mr. Godfrey Wyndham to join the frigate *Mermaid*, Captain Maitland, ordered to the Channel, there to do the service of a midshipman. Angel's voice sounded to herself rather strange and far-away as she asked:

'When does the *Mermaid* sail?'

'In four days. Captain Maitland is in London; he'll be here to-morrow. I have sent for Godfrey. But dear me, dear me, Angelica, he seems very young, very young!'

And Angel said, in the same quiet tones, that Godfrey was nearly fourteen, and how fortunate it was for him to have the chance of being under Captain Maitland; they would be so happy to think of him on board the *Mermaid*. And when she went to find Betty, Mr. Crayshaw took off his spectacles and wiped them and remarked, as he had done on that past Christmas Day:

'Angelica is a good girl, a very good girl!'

After that there was no time at all for thinking. Angel said afterwards that her head seemed to be quite full of nothing but Godfrey's shirts, and a very good thing it was for all of them. Only while she stitched and sorted and packed, she had all the time a feeling that she ought to be saying something to Godfrey now, before he went out into the great terrible world of which she knew so little, something that would help him and strengthen him in the days to come. But there never came a minute for saying it until the very last evening, when Godfrey's box was packed, and his last visits paid in the village, where the old women cried over him in his uniform. The captain had gone for a walk with Mr. Crayshaw, Penny was getting supper ready, and Angel and Betty and Godfrey found themselves together in the garden, really with nothing more to do.

It was the twilight hour, which the two young aunts had always given up to Godfrey. Betty used to look grave about it in the old days, and say she was afraid it was very idle; but she always gave in, and joined Angel and Godfrey when they paced up and down the garden walk, or sat in Miss Jane's arbour, or watched the stars come out from the parlour window, or squeezed into the big arm-chair before the fire. They were in the garden this evening, for it was mild and still, with autumn scents in the air and stars coming out behind a misty haze. And now surely was the time for the last words, the tender advice and warnings that were to go with Godfrey out into the world. But somehow Angel and Betty never spoke them after all. Instead they talked about the past; of Godfrey's first coming to Oakfield—'horrid little wretch that I was,' said the nephew—with the curly head, which had only reached Angel's elbow then, rubbing fondly against her shoulder; of Kiah's coming home, and the captain's first visit, and that Christmas party at the Place.

'And do you remember,' Godfrey said, 'that first day I settled to be a sailor?'

'The Sunday afternoon when we saw Kiah? Yes, of course I do, Godfrey. I never dreamed when we went up to the Place that day what it would put into your head.'

'It wasn't only going to the Place,' said Godfrey thoughtfully; 'I don't know whether I should have settled like that if you hadn't said that to me before.'

'Said what, Godfrey? I don't remember.'

'Don't you, Aunt Angel? I do, every word; about being useful and making the world a bit better. I knew then I'd got to do it, and it was only to settle how; and when I heard about Kiah and the captain, I thought it seemed the nicest way, and I knew it would please you. And it does, doesn't it? That's the best part of going, knowing you're glad for me to go.'

Angelica's hand met Betty's in the dusk and held it tight, and for once it was she who answered for them both:

'Yes, Godfrey dear, very glad and very proud.'

'I told the captain so yesterday,' Godfrey went on; 'and he said I'd better make up my mind directly to be a hero, for I came of an heroic family. That was what he said, and I sha'n't forget. There's the captain and Cousin Crayshaw.'

'Yes, go and meet them,' Angel said, for Betty's hand was trembling in her own and she could hear the catch in her breath that meant she was strangling her tears. She slipped her hand out of Godfrey's arm and let him go forward, while she and Betty drew back through the gap in the yew hedge to Miss Jane's arbour, just where Betty had flung herself down in despair on that first day of Godfrey's coming to Oakfield. They were almost the same words that she gasped out now on Angel's shoulder, as they sat down on the bench side by side; for Betty, though she was nineteen now and wore her hair in a knot at the top of her head, and considered herself a rather elderly person, was much the same vehement little lady as the Betty we knew at thirteen.

'I can't do it,' she sobbed, 'I can't, it's no use; I'm not the right person to be—to be a hero's aunt. I don't want him to go, I shall die if he gets killed; I sha'n't be proud, I shall only be miserable; what am I to do?'

Angel's arms tightened their clasp, she bent her head low over Betty's fair hair and tried to speak once or twice in vain. Then she said at last:

'Dear, we must just say what we said the first day he came. We want to love him, not our own pleasure in him; we haven't loved him and prayed about him and tried to teach him just for ourselves.'

'Oh, I don't know,' faltered Betty; 'I'm afraid I'm selfish, I'm not brave like you. I thought I should feel like the Spartan mothers, but I don't. I can't think of the country. I can only think of Godfrey.'

'Oh, Betty dear, I'm not brave—I never was. I don't feel a bit like a Spartan mother; but it seems to me we needn't mind about what we feel like. We've only got to try and look brave and help poor Cousin Crayshaw, for he is dreadfully sad, and make it easy for Godfrey to go, and not let him think we're fretting.'

'But if we can't?' sighed Betty.

'Do you remember what Martha said the first day?—"We never have a job given us that's too hard for us to do." What do you think, Betty dear, ought we to go in now?'

As they came through the gap in the hedge they nearly ran into the captain in the dusk. He half hesitated, as if unwilling to speak, and then wished them good-night.

'Oh, but you're coming to supper, Captain Maitland,' said Betty. 'Cousin Crayshaw and all of us expected you.'

'I think I must say good-night, Miss Betty,' the captain said a little hesitatingly; 'I—I shall have a good deal to do this evening.'

'Oh, but I know your packing doesn't take long,' said Betty eagerly; 'please do come.'

They both guessed that he was going home to a lonely evening because he would not intrude upon their last night with Godfrey, and they couldn't let him do that.

'I know Cousin Crayshaw expects you,' urged Angel, 'and Godfrey will be so pleased too.'

And Betty, growing bold in the darkness, added earnestly: 'And if you are thinking about Angel and me, it makes it easier for us to pretend to be brave, though we aren't in the least, when you are there.'

The captain did not answer for a minute, and when he did his voice had a strange tremor in it.

'You know,' he said, 'that anything that I can do for you or for Godfrey, anything that is in my power, it will be my greatest happiness to do. I have wanted to say this before Godfrey and I sailed together, and I know you will understand, and not overrate my power to help him and care for him.'

The next minute he had a hand of each of the girls.

'We know you love him almost as much as we do,' said Betty's eager voice.

'And it is our greatest comfort in the world just now to think that he will be with you,' added Angel's gentle tones.'

108

'And you'll come to supper and help us, won't you?' urged Betty. And so the captain came, and what a help he was! How he seemed to know just when to be silent, and when it would help them all most for him to talk! And though he didn't often talk about his own doings, he told them this evening a good deal about his last cruise, when he had been to the West Indies, where Godfrey was born. And he tried to find out how much Godfrey remembered of the country, and spoke of how English people always draw together in a foreign land, and are kind and friendly to every stranger who speaks their own tongue. There was one man in particular, he said, an Englishman, a successful planter, who had come forward to help him when he was ordered off in a hurry, and was in trouble about one of his midshipmen who was down with the fever.

'He came and took him off my hands,' the captain said, 'and had him into his own house; a man I never set eyes on before, and I don't even so much as know his name. He asked it as a favour, saying he'd no child of his own, nor any kith and kin who cared enough for him to want his help.'

'Poor man! I daresay he was glad enough,' said Angel; while Betty echoed:

'Poor man, fancy having no one belonging to him!'

For it would be better, she thought, to break one's heart over such a parting as was to come next day, than to have no one in the world from whom parting would be pain. And really the thought of that lonely Englishman in the far-away island helped her a little over letting Godfrey go.

It was strange that when he really was gone the most restless person in Oakfield was Kiah, who all those years had been so busy and contented at the Place. He took to hobbling up and down the garden path instead of sitting on his bench or by the fire, leaning over the gate and scanning the country, as if he were watching for the French to come, and presenting himself daily at the cottage to know if they had any news of the young master.

And at last, about a month after the *Mermaid* had sailed, he came one day in his best clothes and with a bundle in his hand, looking more cheery than he had done since Godfrey left.

'Yes, young ladies,' he said, as Angel and Betty asked wonderingly where he was going, 'I'm off down South for a bit of a visit. I bean't tired of Oakfield, nor I don't look for no home but here among my folks, but it's come over me as I must have a blow o' the sea and a sight of a ship again, and Timothy Blake, that was an old messmate o' mine, I give him my word I'd see him one o' these days, and I've a many friends beside him on the Devon coast. And then you see, young ladies, I might be getting a sight o' the *Mermaid*.'

'O Kiah!' gasped Betty, as if she longed to ask him to take her too.

'But are you going alone, Kiah?' asked Angel.

'Trust an old salt to take care of himself, Miss Angel. Ay, and if Boney ever gets ashore down there, which ain't likely, but just might be, I'd like to be near about, so I would, for I haven't forgotten how to fire a gun; a hand and a half's good enough for that.'

'And what does Martha say?' asked Betty.

Kiah chuckled.

'She's a wise one, is our Martha. She says she always knew I was a bit of a rolling stone, and my chair'll just be waiting against I come in again.'

And so the little Oakfield world had a fresh, interest in the great world's doings, and Nancy, at any rate, felt that they might all laugh at the notion of a French invasion, with the captain and Mr. Godfrey in the Channel, and Uncle Kiah keeping guard on shore.

CHAPTER VIII

IN THE CHANNEL

'Britannia needs no bulwarks,
    No towers along the steep:
Her march is o'er the mountain waves,
    Her home is on the deep.'—CAMPBELL.

ne spring afternoon a gentleman was strolling along the cliff path which led to a little fishing village on the Devonshire coast, some miles from Plymouth. He seemed to be in no particular hurry, and indeed to have no special destination, for he stopped once or twice and looked about him, and turned off a little way into the fields as if he were exploring a country that was new to him.

Presently he came in sight of an old man with a wooden leg, who was standing near the edge of the cliff, scanning the wide expanse of dancing water with a telescope. He was so much absorbed in what he was looking at that he never noticed the stranger until he was close to him, when he touched his hat and wished him good-day.

'You are on the look-out for some ship?' said the gentleman, following the direction of the old man's eyes.

'Ay, sir, but my sight ain't what it was. I could have vowed I saw a sail yonder, but I can't be sure. Take a look, will you kindly, sir? Your eyes are a deal younger than mine.'

The new-comer took the glass accordingly, but though his eyes were younger they had had less practice than the old sailor's, and he was obliged to own that he could see nothing.

'You are more used to looking out for ships than I am,' he said, as he gave the glass back.

'Ay, sir, I was afloat, boy and man, over fifty year, and good for a few year more if the "froggies" had left me my leg. They want men with all their limbs, you see, in these times, though I'm seaworthy yet, I fancy, and if Boney ever got ashore here, I'd let 'em know I'd my arms still.'

'And so you've settled down at home here,' said the stranger, throwing himself down on the short green turf.

'Well, my home ain't just here, sir, so to speak. My folks live further inland, but now and again I get a longing for a breath o' salt, and an old messmate of mine here has given me a corner for a bit. For you see, sir, the old ship's in the Channel now, and one might hear something of her any day, or maybe see her even; and what's more, the captain's got our boy with him, you see.'

'Your son, do you mean?'

'No, no, sir, I'm a single man, and this here's a quarter-deck young gentleman, and will make as fine an officer as any in the service. And when I said to our Miss Angel that I was thinking of coming down here for a bit, where I could keep an eye on him, as it might be, I could see she was pleased. And so here I am and on the look-out, for the captain might be bringing in a prize any day, none more likely, and then I'd make a shift to get in to Plymouth and see them both, and there'd be news for the young ladies. But there, sir, you'll forgive me running on like this; they say at home Kiah's the one for a yarn if you've the time to listen; which is my name, sir, Hezekiah Parker, at your service, Kiah for short, so to say, and my parents thinking it maybe be presuming to call a bit of a boy the whole name of a Bible king.'

'Oh, you won't tire me, Kiah,' said the stranger, lying back on the grass with his arms under his head, while he followed with his eyes the flight of a lark up into the untroubled blue sky. 'I've not so many friends to talk to that I get tired of the sound of their voices.'

'You're maybe not from these parts, sir?'

'No, I've been away from England for years,' was the answer. 'I've had some queer ups and downs, and tried being a prisoner, and come very near to leaving my bones in foreign parts.'

Kiah touched his hat with increased respect.

'I ask your pardon, sir. I didn't guess as you'd seen service.'

'No, not your sort of service, Kiah; nothing so fine. I'm nothing grander than a West Indian planter.'

'Well, sir, it's welcome home to you, all the same.'

'Well, I suppose my country is home,' said the stranger, rather sadly, 'but I don't know about the welcome. I've outstayed the time for that, Kiah, and there's no one now will care to see me back.'

'I wouldn't be too sure of that if I was you, sir, especially if you've women folks belonging to you. It's wonderful, sir, how they keep a man's place warm for him, and a deal more than we deserve, I say, that go knocking about the world all our lives, and coming back useless old hulks when we can't do for ourselves any longer. Why, there's my sister Martha, with a man and children of her own to think about, and yet, when I come back with my hand and a half and my timber toe, "Kiah," says she, "you're kindly welcome, so you are, and you shall have a chair by our fire as long as we have a fire ourselves, my dear." And as for our young ladies, I doubt there'll be nobody sit in the young master's place till he comes back himself to fill it.'

'Oh, you and your young master have been good brothers, I daresay,' said the stranger, looking up at the singing lark with rather sad eyes.

'Not so extra particular for me, sir, though Martha and me was good friends enough; and as for the young gentleman, the ladies aren't his sisters but his aunts, you see, he having neither father nor mother, brother nor sister. Bless 'em, they're that wrapped up in him; and yet they haven't spoilt him, not they. "You see, Kiah," Miss Angel says to me, "we feel like as if we must answer to his dear papa, our brother that's dead, for how we bring up his boy; we daren't be pleasing ourselves, Kiah," says she. Dear, now, that's one thing I'm bound to own I miss down here, them coming in and out. But, if you'll believe it, sir, I've got a letter Miss Angel wrote me herself. I got my mate's missus, that's a fine scholar, to write to her for me, and there come a beautiful answer back; leastways them as read it to me says it's written like a book. I can make shift with a chapter of the Bible, but I can't get on with handwriting, you see. But it sounds just like as if she was talking to me, and she sends me a sovereign for a poor soul that lost her husband in a brush in the Channel last month—she's that feeling, Miss Angel, and she knows what it is to have them belonging to her in danger.'

The gentleman put his hand in his pocket.

'I'll give you something for her too,' he said; 'and mind you, Kiah, there's a worse thing than having those belonging to you in danger, and that's to have no one belonging to you at all. I'm staying at Plymouth for a bit, and I shall see you again.'

'Well, I hope you will, sir, and I'm very grateful to you, I'm sure, and so will she be; and you'll make yourself some friends, I doubt, if you be short of relations.'

And then, after fumbling in his pockets, he produced a letter, wrapped up with much care in a sheet of paper.

'May be, sir, you'd like to see the young lady's letter. No, you needn't read it all at once, for you see it's a long letter and very beautiful, and you being a scholar you'll understand that, and if you're coming in to-morrow you'd bring it back to me.'

The stranger promised and put the precious paper in his pocket, and then strolled away along the cliffs.

He had nowhere particular to go and nothing particular to do, only he liked to be out here, where the breeze blew salt and fresh in his face, and where he could see the dancing, plunging waves, and the beautiful line of coast. He had had plenty of hard work in the last few years, and had been tired and ill when he started a few months before for the country which, as he had said to Kiah, must always be home.

And now he found himself wondering whether it were worth while to get strong again, and to be brave and successful as he had been lately, when there was no one in all the world to whom his success made any difference. He had grown more happy and hopeful since he had come to Plymouth, for in those days, when the safety of England was depending from hour to hour upon her coast defences, the very life and heart of England seemed to be stirring and throbbing in the great seaport town. Even now, in these happier days, when no hostile ships are waiting for our weak moments in the Channel, we can hardly stand on Plymouth Hoe and see the stately ships in the port, and the guns ready to thunder defiance from the citadel, and think of Drake turning cheerily from his game of bowls to meet the Armada 'For God and Queen Bess,' without thrilling and glowing at the thought of the little land that rules the waves. And in those days every one was so eager and patriotic, and so ready and willing to fight Boney if he came, that our traveller had caught the enthusiasm too, and was wondering how he could give to his country's service the life that seemed of little use to any one else. Here, on the coast, where the danger was most real and present, people drew together in the sympathy of the one great anxiety, and the lonely man felt as if, in coming back to England, he had really got among friends, who were all ready to talk and tell the latest news and discuss the common safety with him as if he were indeed one of themselves.

He liked the fisher folk, too, in the villages round about, they were so frank and simple and kindly; and once or twice he had been out in their boats, for after the hot southern climate he had come from he felt as if he could not have too much of the fresh salt air. And there was always excitement, too, in the Channel in those days, when even a fishing-boat might have to make sail and get away at her best speed before a French privateer.

When he got back to Plymouth late in the evening after his talk with Kiah Parker he found every one in a state of great excitement. The landlady of the lodgings he had taken during his stay there was eager to tell him the latest news. A frigate had come into the port just at sundown with a fine prize—a French gun-brig, taken after a stubborn fight in which both vessels had suffered severely. The first lieutenant had brought the ship in, the captain being wounded and disabled, but the whole place was ringing with his praise.

It had been a most brilliant capture, only the greatest daring and most skilful management could have carried it out.

Two brigs had both attacked the English frigate, and she had made a feint of flight and then turned on them and managed to sink one and disable the other. She would have to wait for repairs. So much the good landlady had told before her lodger could ask a question, and when she paused for breath he inquired whether she knew the name of the English ship. Certainly, the *Mermaid* frigate, Captain Maitland; heaven send he was not badly hurt, poor gentleman! Had there been any loss? Not many killed, she thought, a matter of one or two men, and one officer downed, but a many wounded, they were in hospital; and she branched off into stories of sailor friends of her own, while her lodger tried to remember why the name of the ship and the captain were so familiar to him. It came back to him later in the evening, when he was reading his paper after a solitary supper. It was a midshipman of the *Mermaid* whom he had nursed in a fever in his far-away West Indian home, and it was the praises of Captain

Maitland that the lad was always singing. What a pleasant visitor he had been! What a regretful longing he had left behind him for such another blithe stout-hearted English boy who might call that house his home! His late host wondered if he were in Plymouth, and decided to try and find him out next morning, but one of his fishermen friends came to invite him to go on a two days' cruise, and he accepted readily.

It was a bright day, but there were clouds on the horizon and a fresh breeze springing up; there might be a capful of wind at night, the fisherman said, but the gentleman didn't mind that, he knew. The gentleman said he would like it all the better, and he won the men's hearts as they went along before the wind by his questions about navigation, about rocks and shoals and sandbanks, and the adventures which they were ready enough to tell over again. And their guest had stories of his own to tell, about marvellous adventures with mutinous slaves in the West Indies, and of how he had escaped from their hands to be taken by a French privateer, and was freed by a storm in which the ship went down. And in the interest of the tales and the weather and the fishing he almost forgot about the excitement of the day before, for the bringing in of a prize was a common enough event in war time.

In the afternoon the wind freshened to something like a gale; the fishermen were too busy and alert for talk, and their guest was left to his own thoughts. And then he found himself going back to his conversation with the old sailor. What a good cheery old fellow he was, and what a happy view of life he managed to take after all his ups and downs! And one piece of advice which he had given so frankly to his new acquaintance kept running in the stranger's head, it had been there ever since, though he wouldn't let himself think of it. 'It's wonderful,' Kiah had said, 'how women folks keep a man's place warm for him,' and involuntarily he found himself thinking how it would be if he should test the old man's words on his own account.

'No, it's nonsense for me,' he thought; 'she probably doesn't remember that she ever saw me, and since then she can't have heard very attractive accounts. No, no, better not turn up to be an embarrassment to them if they're alive, for even that I don't know.'

Just then one of the fishermen caught his attention by a remark to his companion: 'Ay, poor old Kiah'll take it hard, such a work as he made about him; but after all he couldn't look for better, only it's hard like when the young uns go.'

'Do you know Kiah Parker?' asked the stranger.

'Ay, surely sir, everybody knows Kiah. Poor old chap, he'll be breaking his heart over his young master, as he calls him, for I doubt 'twas him was drowned off the *Mermaid* in the tussle the other day.'

'Drowned, was he? Is it certain?' asked the visitor, with sudden interest.

'Ay, so they say, not a doubt of it. It's a pity, he was as smart a middy as any afloat, so they say. I saw the bo's'un myself, that was piping his eye like a baby to think of him safe ashore and the lad at the bottom.'

The stranger did not answer. His thoughts had flown to Kiah's young ladies, waiting and watching at home for the boy whom no favouring wind would blow home to them. How strange it seemed, he thought, that that young life should be cut off when so many would mourn for it, and that he, whose life or death made no difference to any one, should have come safely through so many strange accidents and changes and chances of fortune! And then he suddenly remembered that letter which Kiah had given him, and which had been in his pocket unthought of ever since. He felt as if he hardly liked to look at it now, as if it were presumption to read the words of one on whom so terrible a grief had fallen. But he took it out of his pocket, and unfolded it from its wrapping, and glanced at the beginning by the red light of the stormy sunset which beginning to blaze in the western sky. And as he did so the heading caught his eye: 'Oakfield Cottage.'

He gave a great start, and half dropped the closely-written sheet. And then he laughed at himself. There might be other Oakfield Cottages in the world besides the one which stirred such a host of boyish memories by the very sound of its name. He turned the letter over to look at the signature. There it was, plain enough in the clear, legible writing:

'Your sincere friend,
    'ANGELICA WYNDHAM.'

The reader put his hand before his eyes for a moment, seeming to feel again a pair of soft arms round his neck, a curly head pressed against his cheek, while a trembling child's voice whispered to him not to cry because they would wake Betty, and papa and mamma would come back. Little Angel, the little sister whom he had never seen but that once when they grew near together in a few minutes under the shadow of a great grief, she might well have grown into such a woman as old Kiah had spoken of with loving pride.

'Boat ahoy!'

The shout came faint and far away across the gleaming tossing water from where that red glow burned in the west. The fishermen were on the look out at once, a hail in those days might mean something serious; but their passenger sat with the letter unread in his hand, unheeding anything, reading instead a page out of the long ago past.

But after a minute or two the fishermen's excited words brought him back to the present.

'Boat? Not a bit of it. 'Tis a bit of a raft, some poor chap on a spar. English too, 'twas an English shout. Well, and if he was Boney himself we're bound to get him aboard.'

'Where is he?' asked the stranger, shading his eyes from the dazzling sun rays.

onder, sir, don't you see him, there, just where you're looking? We'll have him aboard in a minute.'

All eyes were fixed on the black moving object in the water, which, as they came nearer, proved to be a large piece of wreckage to which a figure was clinging. Presently it could be seen that the figure was that of a boy, who seemed to be holding to the tossing spars with the last effort of his strength, for when he was hailed again he made no reply, only lifting his head for a moment.

'He'll hardly get hold of a rope,' said one of the men doubtfully; 'he's about done for, that last hail was as much as he could do.'

The next moment the mass of wreckage disappeared for a moment, and when it rose again there was a cry of dismay from the boat, for the boy was gone. Another minute showed him lifted high on the crest of a wave, and, before any one else could move, the strange gentleman was overboard and striking out boldly towards him. A few breathless moments, then he had hold of him, and immediately a rope, thrown by a powerful arm, struck the water close to them. It was the work of a minute to knot it about his waist, and he and his unconscious burden were dragged on board amid the congratulations of the fishermen.

'Well done, sir! Didn't know you could swim like that. Never gave us a chance, no more you did. Take a sup o' this,' and a can was put to his lips; 'never mind about the lad, he'll do well enough. Lift his head a bit, Jack, and loose his jacket. What's that bag hung round his neck? Why, bless us, he's an officer, he is—see his clothes; may be 'tis Kiah's middy; there'd be a thing if we'd picked him up!'

'He's alive, isn't he?' gasped the stranger.

'Alive, sir? Bless you, yes! he's coming round this minute; give us the can there, Tom; turn his face this way. How now, sir; won't you live to drub the "froggies" again, eh?'

Even as he spoke the boy's eyelids fluttered, and then a pair of wide grey eyes looked wonderingly round the group. He closed them again, drew a long breath, and then looked about him with understanding coming back to his face.

'Where am I?' he asked, and at the same moment his fingers seemed to be seeking for something.

'Aboard the *Elizabeth* of Plymouth, sir, thanks to this here gentleman that took to the water for you when you and your raft parted company. Is it a bit of a leather bag you might be looking for, sir?'

'Yes, is it here?' said the boy eagerly, and trying to lift his head; 'there are French papers in it, despatches I think. I dived after them when they threw them overboard; I kept them as dry as I could.'

'Safe they are, sir, and wonderful dry considering,' said one of the men after a hasty examination.

'You bean't the young gent from the *Mermaid* frigate, I suppose?' said another, pushing his head into the group.

'I'm Godfrey Wyndham, H.M.S. *Mermaid*', said the boy faintly, and then, with sudden eagerness, 'Do you know anything about her?'

'Safe in Plymouth, sir, with a nice prize behind her. Every one taking on fine about you, sir.'

'Thank God!' the boy said simply and reverently. At the same moment there was an exclamation:

'What's wrong with the gentleman?'

The stranger had pushed his way through the group and was leaning over the boy, looking whiter than Godfrey himself, and with a strange hungry gaze in his eyes. The kindly fishermen took hold of him, for he was trembling from head to foot.

'You let him be, sir, he'll do all right. Come you below and have a drop o' something, you're dead beat. There, sir, let him be a bit, and he'll talk to you fast enough. He's a tough little heart of oak, he is; let him be a bit and he'll do.'

'What did he say his name was?' said the stranger, kneeling down by the young midshipman and trying to steady his voice.

The fishermen shook their heads; they didn't rightly catch, only he belonged to the *Mermaid*, they were sure of that. Did the gentleman know him?

'I am not sure; perhaps I do,' said the stranger briefly, and he made a movement as if to carry the boy down to the cabin himself. Two or three pairs of stout arms were ready to help him, and plenty of hearty voices to assure him that the young gentleman would be all right; they'd get his wet clothes off and let him sleep, he was bound to be about done; he'd be all right in no time. And Godfrey fulfilled their prediction by sinking into the sound healthy sleep of a tired boy, with a dreamy sense of satisfaction that the *Mermaid* and the despatches were all safe. But the strange gentleman did not take the advice of his hosts and follow the boy's example. All that night he spent awake and watchful by Godfrey's side. He had had a good many hard hours in his life, but none that seemed quite so long as those night hours in the narrow cabin of the fishing smack, while the boat rocked on the heaving Channel, and the swinging lamp over his head showed him the sleeping face of the young sailor to whom the sound of wind and waves was the most familiar lullaby. How he studied the still young face by the uncertain light, trying to trace in the broad-chested sturdy midshipman some memory of a white-faced eager little boy who had once looked up wonderingly into his own sad eyes! And if he turned his eyes from him for a moment, it was to decipher by the dim lamplight that letter of Kiah's with the heading and the signature that were so familiar. And when the agony of uncertainty grew almost unbearable, he dropped his head in his hands by the boy's side with the half-stifled murmur:

'If it might be—far, far beyond my deserving—but if it might be!'

He scarcely noticed how the grey light of dawn grew stronger about them, how the gale dropped and the boat sped along before a steady breeze, until Godfrey suddenly opened his eyes and looked up with the puzzled wondering gaze that thrilled the watcher through and through with vivid recollection.

'I know I'm not on board the *Mermaid*' he said, 'but I can't remember how I came here, and what boat this is.'

'You are on board a fishing smack from Plymouth,' said the stranger, struggling hard to speak calmly; 'you were picked up last night clinging to some wreckage in mid-Channel.'

Godfrey's face brightened with quick understanding.

'I know, I know,' he said, 'and the papers are all right, and the *Mermaid* too. That's the last thing I remember. I feel as if I'd been asleep for weeks. I wonder if I shall get long enough leave to run home, it would be rare to tell them all?' Then looking up doubtfully at his companion, he added:

'I'm sure I ought to know you, sir; I beg your pardon, but I can't put your name to you.'

'Where do you think you have seen me?' asked the stranger eagerly.

'I don't remember, sir. It's very stupid of me. Is—is anything wrong, sir? Can I do anything?'

'Yes,' cried the stranger, with his self-control breaking down, 'you can tell me in mercy the name of your father.'

'My father's name was Bernard Wyndham,' said Godfrey wonderingly. 'He was killed in the West Indies some years ago. I say, what is it, sir—you're ill, aren't you? I'll fetch— —'

But the stranger had fast hold of him.

'Don't fetch any one,' he gasped, 'I want you, only you. Godfrey, my boy, my son, look at me, don't quite forget me—you say you've seen me before! Godfrey, believe me—don't say you can't believe me, my boy, my only child!'

The colour rushed into Godfrey's face.

'I—I don't understand,' he faltered. 'Why didn't you come?'

'Because I thought you were dead, my little boy; because they told me every one died together, and you too. Because when I got free and came back they showed me the graves and told me yours was one.'

Still Godfrey held back doubtfully, though the pale eager face was so strangely familiar.

'But why didn't you come home?' he asked; 'they've been so unhappy about you, the aunts have. Why didn't you let them know?'

'Because I was a coward, Godfrey; because I never knew they cared for me—why should they? Ay, and why should you?'

He had turned his head away, when he suddenly felt himself seized in such an embrace as Godfrey generally kept for Angel and Betty.

'Father,' cried the eager young voice, 'papa, I'm a brute, I didn't understand! I know you now—I half knew you all the time. Why, they've talked about you all these years, they never let me forget. I say, I mustn't make a baby of myself, I'm an officer, you know, but it makes one feel as if one was standing on one's head to think of bringing you home to them.'

And I don't think that Godfrey disgraced the King's uniform, even if he laid his curly head down on his new found father's shoulder and hugged him as he hugged his Aunt Angel.

CHAPTER IX

IN PORT

'If conquering and unhurt I came
Back from the battle-field,
It is because thy prayers have been
My safeguard and my shield.'—A. A. PROCTER.

nd meanwhile how had it been at Oakfield, little Oakfield, which had its share in the joys and sorrows of those stirring times? Angel and Betty could hardly remember afterwards exactly how they heard the news; it seemed to be all over the place directly, and no one could have said who actually told it. But it was Mr. Crayshaw who brought it—poor Mr. Crayshaw, so aged and altered and broken-down that to care for him and comfort him seemed the first thing his two young cousins had to do and to think of. And indeed with Angel it was so much more natural to think of other people first that she seemed to feel Godfrey's loss chiefly in the way in which it would affect them all— Cousin Crayshaw, who had had to meet the first shock of the news; poor old Penny; Nancy, who had been his playfellow; Betty above all, who had said she could never bear it if Godfrey died for his country. Poor Betty made such desperate efforts to be brave and unselfish, choked back her tears so manfully, faltered such bold words about their boy having died as he would have wished for King and Country. And then she would run away and sob passionately over Godfrey's toy boats, the lesson-books he had used with her, the bed he had slept in, and then would tell herself she was not worthy of him, and come back to be brave and self-controlled before the others once more. While Angel, for her part, hardly expected to be ever worthy of her boy, only went her quiet way,

cried bitterly on Martha's shoulder, sat on a stool at Cousin Crayshaw's feet as if she were a little girl again, and did the work which Penny forgot, and found comfort somehow from them all. Angel could not be Betty, and Betty could not be Angel, no two people meet joy and sorrow and do their brave, unselfish deeds in just the same way; and the beautiful part is that there is room on the great list of honour for the Betties who school themselves to courage, and the Angels who are simply brave in their self-forgetfulness, and the world is the better for them both.

It was three days after the news had come—Angel and Betty unconsciously counted the time like that now, looking back to the days when they didn't know that Godfrey was dead as to something beautiful and far away.

Angel was in the garden, sitting with her work in Miss Jane's arbour. There was so much work to be done, and poor old Penny cried so bitterly over the black stuff that her damp needle and thread didn't get on very fast, and Angel took it quietly away from her and carried it out of doors. Penny had a sort of idea that there was something wrong in sewing at mourning dresses in the garden, but Angel thought it didn't matter. Betty felt as if the glory of the spring-time, the flowers in the borders and the birds' song and the vivid green of the meadows, were like a mockery of their grief, but to Angel the sunny sweetness brought a strange comfort which she did not try to understand. Martha had promised to come round and help her, but it was afternoon now and she had not come. She was very busy at home, Angel supposed, but still it was not like her not to keep an appointment when she had said she would come. Betty sat on the grass at her sister's feet. She had her work, too, but it did not get on very fast. She laid it down at last and leaned back against the stone shoulder of Demoiselle Jehanne, much as she had been used to do in the days when she was a little girl and used to come to her for comfort. There was something about the peacefulness of the still figure under the flowers which soothed Betty still, she hardly knew how. She remembered, almost with a smile, how Godfrey had always believed that Miss Jane's heart was broken by a naughty nephew, and he had been so afraid of the same thing happening to her and Angel. She had almost come to believe in the story herself, and as her fingers strayed half caressingly over the familiar broken face she wondered how Miss Jane felt when she was a living, loving, sorrowing woman here at Oakfield. Did she know about the dreary blank, the aching longing which had come to the little girls who used to play beside her? And a hundred years hence would it matter as little to any one that Godfrey lay under the tossing Channel waters as it did to-day that a sad woman's heart had broken long ago? A timid step on the path made them look up, and there stood Nancy, waiting with much less assurance than usual for them to notice her. Angel held out her hand.

'Well, Nancy dear,' she said, 'where is your mother?'

Nancy for answer began to cry.

'O Miss Angel, you won't be angry, will you?' she sobbed; 'Patty said I mustn't come, but I couldn't help it, miss.'

'We like you to come, dear,' Angel began gently; but Nancy went on between her sobs:

'It's him—the captain—he's come home, Miss Angel.'

'The captain! When did he come?' cried both the sisters together.

'Last night,' said Nancy, wiping her eyes; 'and, Miss Angel, he's not like the captain a bit now; he looks quite, quite old, and Pete and father they a'most carried him in from the chaise; and do you know, he can't see, he won't be able to see for ever so long, perhaps never. And they told me not to tell you because it'd make you sadder. And this morning he asked me about you, and I said, should I fetch you, and he said, "No, no, you wouldn't want to see him"; but somehow I couldn't help it, and I've come, and, Miss Angel, I'm sure if you saw him you wouldn't be angry with him.'

'Angry!' said Angel, laying her heap of black work down on the arbour seat, 'angry with just the one person we want to see,

Godfrey's best friend, the last person who saw him! You were quite, quite right to come, Nancy dear. Betty, will you — —'

'Come this minute? Of course I will,' said Betty, rising in her old impulsive way. 'Cousin Crayshaw's out, but we can't wait for him, can we, Angel?'

'No, I don't think we can,' said Angel; and in a few minutes the two were walking down the road to the Place, with Nancy, crying still but half-triumphant, between them.

And on the bench outside the house, in Kiah's old place, where Godfrey had first settled to be a sailor, Captain Maitland sat, all alone and not feeling the spring sunshine which fell about him. He hardly knew why he had chosen that place, only just to-day he felt as if, as Nancy said, he had grown old like Kiah, only with none of Kiah's cheery content. His eyes were bandaged from the happy light, but he knew just how it all looked, and he said to himself that it was only he who had changed, not the beautiful, happy world; for he had loved the sunshine, this merry-hearted sailor, and the joy and the beauty of the fair earth, and the stir and the work and bustle of life, and he felt as if it were not himself but some other man who sat here in the darkness at the door of his old home, and as if all his hopeful courage were gone and would never come back. The doctors had told him that he would recover his sight with time and patience; but just now he felt as if he couldn't look forward, only back to that moment which would be before him all his life, the moment when the French brig went down, and he saw his youngest midshipman jump headlong over the side of the *Mermaid*, and knew that his pursuit of the other ship must not be stayed for the sake of one life, and so went on his way, with Angel's white face before his eyes and the sound of Betty's voice in his ears. It was only a few minutes before the shot came which stretched him, blinded and unconscious, on the deck, but they were the sort of minutes in which a man grows old; and when he came to himself, helpless and weak and bewildered, to be told that Godfrey Wyndham had never been seen since the fight, he felt as if the time before were part of another life.

He was wondering sadly this morning why he had hurried home before the doctors wished him to travel; he had been restlessly anxious to get to Oakfield, and now he scarcely knew why. How could he meet Angelica and Betty, when he had come back safe, only useless and helpless, and the boy they had trusted to him, the boy who was the light of their eyes and the joy of their hearts, would never come back to them any more?

And then suddenly a voice sounded close to him; he had been too much taken up with his own thoughts to hear the steps on the path till they were beside him.

'Oh! Captain Maitland'—it was Betty's eager tones—'it is dreadful to see you like this; but you'll be able to see again soon, won't you?'

The captain rose to his feet and stood trembling as he had never trembled before the French guns. And even in the darkness he knew that it was Angel's hand that touched him.

'Please sit down,' she said gently, 'please don't stand. Why did you not let us know? Nancy had to fetch us.'

'How could I?' he said, turning away his face from her, 'how could I, when I would give all the world to be where he is and he here?'

'Oh, we know,' said Betty's earnest voice, 'we both remember what you said, that we mustn't over-rate your power to save him. You don't think we're thinking anything like that, you surely know us better? Angel, Angel, can't you explain?'

'I'm sure Captain Maitland understands,' said Angel very quietly; 'and now he will tell us all about what we most want to hear, we and Cousin Crayshaw and Penny and all—what nobody else can tell us.'

And the captain said 'Yes' as he had said 'Yes' when Angel and Betty fetched him home to help them at supper on the evening before Godfrey went away.

They were all together at the Place that evening, after the captain's story had been told. In spite of the sunny days, the spring nights were chilly, and they gathered round the wood fire in a little panelled room which had been old Mrs. Maitland's sitting-room. It had been scarcely used since, and the lady's things—her favourite chair and her little work-table and her big basket—were still in their places as she had left them, waiting, Martha used to say, like the stores of linen, till the captain brought home his bride. It was Martha who had thought that the big room, which was so full of memories of that merry Christmas party, would seem cold and dreary, and had carried the lamp into the little parlour. And there round the fire they sat together, Betty at Mr. Crayshaw's feet, with his hand caressing her bright hair, and Angel on her low chair beside them, and the captain opposite, with his eyes shaded from the light. Only this evening he had been talking quite hopefully about the time when he would be fit for work again. And they talked about Godfrey too, Angel being the one to begin, and for once it was she who led the talk, and dwelt quite quietly and naturally on old days—on Godfrey's first coming home, and the day when he had first heard Kiah's stories and settled to be a useful sailor. And she spoke freely as she had never done before of hers and Betty's fears and misgivings about his education.

'Don't you remember that first day, Betty, how you said you could never be a maiden aunt? And afterwards, when we knew he was set on being a great sailor, I was more afraid still, for I couldn't think how I was ever to teach him.'

'And little enough help from those who should have been the first to help you,' sighed Mr. Crayshaw.

'Oh no, no—I didn't mean that. Only, you see, we had more to do with him than any one. But Martha was so good, she told us not to worry too much, only to do our best and trust about him. Do you know, I think if I had known then that he would die like this, such a brave, good little officer, I should have felt quite glad and thankful.'

'A gentleman wants to see Miss Wyndham,' said Patty at the door.

'Miss Wyndham cannot see any one to-night,' said Mr. Crayshaw, impatiently.

'Oh yes, I can,' said Angel rising, 'only I don't know who it can be. Where is he, Patty?'

'I showed him into the dining-room, Miss Angelica; he came on here from the cottage, he says.'

Angel went out of the room and across the hall to the dining-room; the front door was open, and across the still meadows the church bells were ringing, for the news of a victory in the Peninsula had reached the village that evening. Angel wondered as she listened if there were many in England who heard through the joyous peal the sound of a bell tolling for some one whose life or death meant more to them than victory or defeat.

'God help them all!' she whispered to herself, for she was one of those whose tender sympathy grows wider at the touch of their own sorrow.

The dining-room was almost dark. Patty had put a candle on the table, but its rays hardly reached the end of the room. The shutters were not closed, and outside it was starlight, as it had been on that Christmas night when she and Godfrey and the captain looked at the Plough shining over the homes of Oakfield. The strange visitor was standing by the table. He turned when Angel came in and gave a great start as he saw her standing there in the doorway, dressed as she had been when Godfrey saw her first, in a white gown with black ribbons, and with the chain round her neck on which she always wore the miniature of her brother. He did not speak, so she said:

'You wished to see me, sir?'

'Yes,' began the stranger hurriedly; 'you are Miss Wyndham, I am sure—Miss Angelica Wyndham. I came—I wished—I once knew some relatives of yours in the West Indies.'

'My brother,' said Angel, faltering a little. Was this a friend of Bernard's come to ask for Godfrey?—and Godfrey was gone.

'Your brother, yes; I knew him very well.'

'He was killed in a rising of the slaves nine years ago,' said Angelica.

'I know his death was reported,' said the stranger; 'there were many killed, and some—some who had marvellous escapes, and returned to find their friends dead, or believed to be dead, and themselves perhaps forgotten.' Something more in the tone than in the words thrilled Angel strangely. She began to tremble.

'Please tell me what you mean,' she said, and she tried to see her visitor's face, but his back was to the light and he stood in deep shadow.

'Some of those supposed to be lost came back,' he said, and his voice faltered too.

Angel put out her hand.

'You have something to tell me,' she said, leaning back against a high carved arm-chair.

The next moment his arm was supporting her, his voice, hoarse and broken, was in her ear.

'Angelica—Angel, do you not understand? Can you remember, can you forgive, do you think? I never guessed that you would care. I thought only to bring trouble if I came. Will you try and forgive me now?'

Angel stood half stunned for a minute leaning against his shoulder, and then suddenly the thought of what might have been swept over her, a bitterness of grief which she had never known before seemed to crush her down. She burst out into passionate crying, such tears as she had never shed.

'Oh, Bernard! Oh, Bernard!' she sobbed, 'we have not got him for you; if you had come—if you had come before—but he is not here any more.'

There was a sound of doors opening, of voices outside; the peal of the church bells rose and fell on the breeze. Angel felt herself drawn into her brother's arms. His voice sounded above her:

'Angel, don't cry so; look up, dear, listen—there are wonders on sea as well as on land; you must listen and hope, and — —'

But at that moment there was a shriek in the hall—Betty's voice, and then a clamour of crying and laughing and questioning, a door burst open, a pair of arms round Angel's neck, a curly head against her cheek, and over all the triumphant tones of Kiah Parker's voice as he stumped with his wooden leg upon the floor.

'Don't you be afeard. Our young ladies ain't the sort as dies of joy, bless 'em, bless 'em all, every one of 'em!' and round the group he hobbled in a sort of Indian war-dance, till Nancy, who couldn't get into the circle and wanted to say something, called out between laughing and crying:

'Oh, Uncle Kiah, do mind the polished floor!'

And all the time the bells rang their cheery peal for what brave English hearts had done.

It was very early the next morning, when only the birds, who scarcely seem to sleep at all in springtime, and the busiest people in Oakfield were up, that Peter Rogers might have been seen setting a ladder against Sir Godfrey's oak-tree and preparing to go up it. Mr. Collins came to the inn door while he was doing it.

'Holloa! Pete, my man, and what may you be after?' he exclaimed.

'Just running a bit of a flag up on the old tree, Mr. Collins, with your good leave.'

Mr. Collins rubbed his hands with great satisfaction.

'And that's quite right to be sure, and very suitable to the occasion, Pete,' he said. 'Bless your heart, who ever looked to see this day when you went up that same tree to get Mr. Godfrey down; and a very near thing too, so it was?'

'To think of me ever having to help Mr. Godfrey down,' laughed Pete, as he lashed the flag-staff to the topmost bough; 'why, if one's to believe Uncle Kiah, he can a'most run up the mast with his eyes shut, and stand on his head on the top.'

'Oh, that's not nearly all he can do,' said Nancy, who was there, of course, steadying the ladder.

'Nance, is it true that your Uncle Kiah came home in a post chaise with the gentlemen?' asked one of the inn maids.

'Of course it is,' said Nancy, with her head inches higher than usual.

'And did King George really thank Master Godfrey himself for saving them French papers?'

'Of course,' said Nancy, promptly, 'or at least he sent somebody very grand to do it.'

'And did he and his papa really swim over from France with the letters in their mouths and the cannon-balls flying all over them?'

'I'll tell you all about it by-and-bye, I'm going to get eggs for the captain's breakfast,' said Nancy, who was as important as the Admiral of the Fleet; 'but you see if Mr. Godfrey doesn't have a ship of his own directly, and medals all over him.'

And at the top of Sir Godfrey's oak the English flag flew free and fair, as it flies amidst the storm of shot and shell, the roar of winds and the din of battle.

It was flying gaily when a party of three came past on their way from the cottage to the Place, Mr. Wyndham, with Betty on one side of him and Godfrey on the other. Betty pointed up into the tree. 'That's where the bough was, Bernard, just under the flag, where Godfrey sat that first day when he was a little naughty boy and I was a little stupid aunt.'

'And you did name me after the great Sir Godfrey, didn't you?' said the young sailor eagerly.

'I named you after the Sir Godfrey of the oak, with some sort of hope, I think, that you might stand under it one day. I'm afraid I didn't think of choosing you an illustrious namesake; I never knew that he did anything particular, except plant that acorn.'

'No more did I,' laughed Betty. 'Don't look horrified, Godfrey; you and I romanced about him so much that I came to think he was a great hero, just as I believed Miss Jane was a broken-hearted aunt.'

'He was my first hero,' Godfrey said, 'before Kiah and the captain came. I shall go on believing in him; he left something good behind him at all events. Do you remember how cross I was because you wouldn't let him sit under his own oak-tree? Oh, there's old Mrs. Ware, I must speak to her; don't wait, I'll catch you.'

He darted off, and the others went on slowly.

Presently Betty said:

'I have been thinking that sometimes people are allowed to sit under their own trees after all, to see the end of what they do. When I look at Godfrey, and think about how we planned for him, it seems so much, much more than I deserve; do you know what that feels like, Bernard?'

'Betty, when I think of you two, keeping the remembrance of a good-for-nothing brother all these years and training up for me such a son as this is, and set that against my deserts, I'm not sure how I could bear the shame of it if the thankfulness were not greater still.'

'Oh hush! you're not to talk like that any more, at any rate not to me. I never should have done anything by myself, it was Angel who settled first of all that we were to be good sisters. And then we thought that was over, and we had to begin to be maiden aunts, and Martha told us not to be afraid, for we never had a job set us without strength to do it. I've made lots of mistakes, I'm not a perfect maiden aunt even now, but Angel might have been born one. Bernard, why are you laughing? I expect you think me a dreadful rattle, but, indeed, I'm much older than I look. Here we are and here's Martha. Good morning, Martha, is the captain up?'

'Up! Why, Miss Betty, my dear, he's gone by the fields to the cottage this half-hour since.'

'All alone? Oh, Martha, that's very rash!' exclaimed Betty in her motherly way. 'Over the brook with no one to lead him! Suppose he missed his footing?'

'Oh, the captain's sight's a deal better this morning,' said Martha, with her broadest smile. 'I don't think he'll come to any harm, Miss Betty.'

'Well, we'll go after him,' Betty said, 'or we may meet him coming back; for I do think it's rash, Martha, I do indeed!'

But Martha only went on smiling as if she were not at all alarmed. So Betty and her brother, with Godfrey following them, went across the meadows by the foot-path to the cottage. And about half way they met the captain, walking erect and strong like his old self, and Angel beside him. And Betty, who had never thought much whether her sister were pretty or not, gave quite a start of surprise, for Angel looked so beautiful at that moment that she wondered why she had never noticed it before. And the captain looked quite radiantly happy, and altogether forgot to say good morning.

'We've been to look for you at the Place,' Betty said; 'and Martha told us you'd gone out all by yourself, and I rather scolded her for letting you; but really I don't think you look as if you wanted taking care of.'

'Don't you?' said the captain; and then he and Mr. Wyndham and Angel suddenly burst out laughing together, Angel with her fair face growing rosy red and the happiest light in her eyes. But the captain took hold of Betty's hand.

'You must try and forgive me, Miss Betty,' he said, 'but I want taking care of so much that I have found a guardian angel for myself who says she will take me in hand.'

And then Angel put her arms round her sister and whispered:

'Betty dear, you will be glad, won't you? And now you'll have two brothers instead of one.'

And Betty stood still a minute while this new wonder grew clear to her, and then threw one arm round Angel and held out the other hand to the captain, and exclaimed at the same moment:

'Oh, Angel, when I was just telling Bernard that you were born to be a maiden aunt!'

The worst of it was, as both Betty and Godfrey declared, that nobody would say they were surprised. Cousin Crayshaw looked as knowing as possible and called Betty 'Mrs. Blind Eyes'; Martha Rogers would do nothing but laugh and say she had made an extra stock of lavender bags last year, knowing Miss Angelica was partial to them. As for Kiah, he frankly declared that he had settled the match years ago.

'No, nor you mustn't take it presuming, Miss Betty,' he said as he sat on his bench, chopping away at a clothes-peg for Martha as if he had never been away, 'but one couldn't but be looking about for a good wife for the captain, and who should one pitch on but the young mistress, that's just built for an admiral's lady, so she is.'

'Oh, then the wedding's to wait for my promotion, Kiah?' said the captain.

'Not a bit of it, captain! Wedding first and cocked hat after, and, mark me, it'll come the quicker for it, asking your pardon, Miss Angel, and no offence meant.'

'Offence! no, I'm very much obliged to you, Kiah,' said Angelica, sitting down beside the old sailor; 'I was only afraid you would think I should spoil the captain for the service.'

'No fear of that, Miss Angel. Some says the best men in a fight must be them as have none at home to think for. They're all out, them folks are. A man serves King and country better for having the right sort o' women folks at home, and he'll go to work the stouter if he keeps his heart warm with a thought o' the mother and sisters behind him.'

'And the aunts, Kiah,' said Godfrey.

'Ay, to be sure, sir, the aunts.'

FINIS

NEW STORY BOOKS FOR THE YOUNG

PUBLISHED BY THE

NATIONAL SOCIETY

BY CHARLOTTE M. YONGE

THE WARDSHIP OF STEEPCOOMBE

By CHARLOTTE M. YONGE, Author of "The Heir of Redclyffe," &c. With Five Full-page Illustrations by W. S.
STACEY. Bevelled boards, cloth gilt, price 3s. 6d. **3/6**

A story of the troublous times of the youth of King Richard II. and of
the work done by Wickliffe and William of Wykeham respectively,
concluding with a graphic and spirited description of Wat Tyler's
rebellion.

BY MARY H. DEBENHAM

THE LAIRD'S LEGACY

By MARY H. DEBENHAM, Author of "Two Maiden Aunts,"
&c. With Three Full-page Illustrations by GERTRUDE
D. HAMMOND. Bevelled boards, cloth gilt, price 2s. 6d. **2/6**

Miss Debenham's new story follows the fortunes of an exiled Scottish
laird, Sir Patrick Maxwell, and his family in France in the early years of
the eighteenth century, and gives some account of the campaigning in the
Low Countries.

BY AUDREY CURTIS

LITTLE MISS CURLYLOCKS

By AUDREY CURTIS, Author of "The Artist of Crooked
Alley," &c. With Two Full-page Illustrations by
GERTRUDE D. HAMMOND. Bevelled boards, cloth gilt,
price 2s. **2/-**

This is a pretty story for young children, and relates how "Little
Miss Curlylocks," living with her high-born grandparents at Montmorency
Manor, becomes acquainted with Alice Fogerty, her brother Tim, and the
Fat Baby, and what happens in consequence.

NATIONAL SOCIETY'S DEPOSITORY, SANCTUARY, WESTMINSTER,

BY KATHERINE E. VERNHAM
A WONDERFUL CHRISTMAS

And other Stories. By KATHERINE E. VERNHAM, Author of "Benedicta's Stranger," &c. With Two Full-page Illustrations by C. J. STANILAND. Bevelled boards, cloth gilt, price 2s.

2/-

A collection of a dozen short stories, dealing for the most part with the waifs and strays to be found in our great cities, and with some of the more admirable points so often to be observed in their characters.

BY G. NORWAY
BESSIE KITSON

By G. NORWAY, Author of "True Cornish Maid," &c. With Two Full-page Illustrations by GERTRUDE D. HAMMOND. Bevelled boards, cloth gilt, price 1s. 6d.

1/6

Bessie Kitson, left an orphan at a very early age, is fortunately rescued from the squalid home in which she has obtained shelter and taken to live with honest, God-fearing people at Windsor. Ultimately the return of Mr. George Kitson from Australia removes all fear of want alike from Bessie and her faithful foster-mother.

BY L. E. TIDDEMAN
TAKING FRENCH LEAVE

By L. E. TIDDEMAN, Author of "Grannie's Treasures," &c. With Two Full-page Illustrations by W. S. STACEY. Bevelled boards, cloth gilt, price 1s. 6d.

1/6

Madge and Will Torrance, the twin children of an artist living in the country, weave a most perplexing web about themselves through playing truant from school on a very hot afternoon ; and their story is likely to prove a useful lesson to other young folks when tempted to be deceitful.

BY CATHERINE P. SLATER
A FRIENDLY GIRL

By CATHERINE P. SLATER, Author of "A Goodly Child," &c. With Frontispiece by C. J. STANILAND. Cloth boards, gilt, price 1s.

1/-

This story describes with much pathos and quiet humour how Jeanie Scott, a member of the Girls' Friendly Society, goes as a "general" servant to Miss Marget Melville, an old maid living in the suburbs of Edinburgh, and of certain things that happened while Jeanie was there.

In addition to the preceding, the following Prize Books are also published by the Society:—

BY CHARLOTTE M. YONGE

Author of "The Heir of Redclyffe," "Cameos from English History," &c.

THE CARBONELS

With Five Full-page Illustrations by W. S. STACEY. Bevelled boards, cloth gilt, price 3s. 6d.

"The Carbonels" deals with the various sides of life in the little village of Uphill Priors in the years immediately following 1822.

"This is altogether a well-written, thoroughly interesting story."
SATURDAY REVIEW.

3/6

THE COOK AND THE CAPTIVE

With Five Full-page Illustrations by W. S. STACEY. Bevelled boards, cloth gilt, price 3s. 6d.

This story is descriptive of life in Gaul in the times of Franks and Burgundians, telling how young Attalus is given as a hostage to a barbarian chief, of the good he is able to effect among his heathen surroundings, and of his rescue and his final escape to his own home.

"A historical romance suited to youthful readers. . . . Told with all the art in narration that Miss Yonge has long been noted for."—RECORD.

3/6

THE TREASURES IN THE MARSHES

With Three Full-page Illustrations by W. S. STACEY. Bevelled boards, cloth gilt, price 2s. 6d.

This tale is concerned with the finding of Anglo-Saxon treasures in marshy land by members of two neighbouring families, and describes the different ways in which the treasures were dealt with and the ultimate consequences.

"Miss Charlotte Yonge describes . . . a variety of family incidents in her inimitable way, drawing lessons so cleverly from her story that young people will remember both the tale and its teaching."—YORKSHIRE POST.

2/6

THE CROSS ROADS

With Five Full-page Illustrations by J. F. WEEDON. Bevelled boards, cloth gilt, price 3s. 6d.

A story of life in domestic service at Langhope Mead, with some amusing sketches of character both in the servants' hall and in the neighbouring village.

"The story is vigorously written throughout, and abounds in amusing incidents and exciting episodes."—EDUCATIONAL TIMES.

3/6

THE CONSTABLE'S TOWER

Or, The Times of Magna Charta. With Four Full-page Illustrations by C. O. MURRAY. Bevelled boards, cloth gilt, price 3s.

A tale of the days of Magna Charta, showing the nobility of the character of Hubert de Burgh, and concluding with a spirited description of the sea-fight off Dover.

"One of the best children's books published this season."—WESTERN ANTIQUARY

3/-

NATIONAL SOCIETY'S DEPOSITORY, SANCTUARY, WESTMINSTER.

BY FRANCES MARY PEARD—*continued*

THE LOCKED DESK

With Five Full-page Illustrations by W. S. STACEY. Bevelled
boards, cloth gilt, price 3s. 6d.

3/6

In this book Miss Peard has left the historical field in which most of
her previous tales for young people have lain, giving us instead a story of
the present day, in which certain documents in Mrs. Barton's locked desk
play an important part.

THE BLUE DRAGON

With Five Full-page Illustrations by C. J. STANILAND.
Bevelled boards, cloth gilt, price 3s. 6d.

3/6

"The Blue Dragon" is the sign of an inn at Chester, where the scene
of the story is laid, in the discontented, turbulent times that followed
immediately upon the battle of Bosworth Field.

"Every page is full of stirring interest."—CHURCH TIMES.

SCAPEGRACE DICK

With Four Full-page Illustrations. Bevelled boards, cloth gilt,
price 3s. 6d.

3/6

A spirited story of adventure in England and the Low Countries in the
days of the Commonwealth.

"A book for boys, which will be read with equal pleasure by their sisters."
PALL MALL GAZETTE.

PRENTICE HUGH

With Six Full-page Illustrations. Bevelled boards, cloth gilt,
price 3s. 6d.

3/6

"Prentice Hugh" gives a graphic account of life during the reign of
Edward the First, mainly in the cathedral city of Exeter.

"Another excellent book. . . . Both boys and girls will enjoy reading 'Prentice
Hugh'; it is in all respects one of the best books of the season."—ST. JAMES'S GAZETTE.

TO HORSE AND AWAY

With Five Full-page Illustrations by C. J. STANILAND.
Bevelled boards, cloth gilt, price 3s. 6d.

3/6

The fortunes of a Royalist family in the times of the Great Civil War
form the leading theme of Miss Peard's story, which, together with many
adventures, gives a few graphic scenes from the life of Charles II. in his
flight from Worcester Field.

"'To Horse and Away' will certainly give pleasure to girls and boys alike."
SATURDAY REVIEW.

NATIONAL SOCIETY'S DEPOSITORY, SANCTUARY, WESTMINSTER.

BY THE AUTHOR OF "MADEMOISELLE MORI" &c

STÉPHANIE'S CHILDREN

3/6 With Five Full-page Illustrations by C. J. STANILAND. Bevelled boards, cloth gilt, price 3s. 6d.

The story of the escape of Stéphanie, a young widow of high family, and her two step-children, from France during the Great Revolution. Descriptive also of the life led among the colony of *émigrés* in London.

"Another proof of the versatility and charm of writing that is already well known in the author of the 'Atelier du Lys,' and will prove a delightful addition to a girl's library."—SATURDAY REVIEW.

NOT ONE OF US

3/6 With Five Full-page Illustrations by J. F. WEEDON. Bevelled boards, cloth gilt, price 3s. 6d.

Descriptive of the career of a young schoolmistress in Northern Italy, and of the manners and customs of the folk dwelling in the valley of Fiorasca.

"This charming picture of Alpine life . . . is as good as anything done by the writer of 'The Atelier du Lys.'"—SPECTATOR.

KINSFOLK AND OTHERS

3/6 With Five Full-page Illustrations by C. O. MURRAY. Bevelled boards, cloth gilt, price 3s. 6d.

A study in the conflicting duties that claim the obedience of Olive Garth, who has been brought up from her earliest days by her grandmother, and whose mother returns from Australia after an absence of seventeen years.

BANNING AND BLESSING

3/6 With Five Full-page Illustrations by C. J. STANILAND. Bevelled boards, cloth gilt, price 3s. 6d.

Descriptive of country life on the confines of wild Dartmoor, at the beginning of the present century. The banning of Lois Smerdon, the black witch, at length comes to an end, and so plentiful are the blessings which follow that all ends happily and full of promise for the future.

"A capital specimen of a book for girls."—SATURDAY REVIEW.

A LITTLE STEP-DAUGHTER

3/6 With Six Full-page Illustrations. Bevelled boards, cloth gilt, price 3s. 6d.

"A Little Step-daughter" is descriptive of life in the South of France in the early part of the eighteenth century.

"The anonymous authoress of 'Mademoiselle Mori' is one of the most delightful of writers for girls. Her books are characterised by a delicacy of touch rarely met with."
—STANDARD.

NATIONAL SOCIETY'S DEPOSITORY, SANCTUARY, WESTMINSTER.

BY M. & C. LEE

Authors of "The Oak Staircase," "Joachim's Spectacles," &c.

MISS COVENTRY'S MAID

With Three Full-page Illustrations by GERTRUDE D. HAMMOND.
Bevelled boards, cloth gilt, price 2s. 6d.

2/6

The identity of Miss Coventry's maid is a mystery to all but her young
mistress, and the mystery remains until after the performance of *She Stoops
to Conquer* at a certain country house where Miss Coventry had been
invited to stay.

"The Misses Lee have hit upon an idea for their story which, as far as we know, is
new. . . . The situation is a good one and is well worked out."—SPECTATOR.

ST. DUNSTAN'S FAIR

With Three Full-page Illustrations by W. S. STACEY. Bevelled
boards, cloth gilt, price 2s. 6d.

2/6

"St. Dunstan's Fair" tells of the folks living in a small country
village in Kent, in the year of Waterloo, of what happened at the Fair
itself, and of the consequences to Nancy Springett and poor George
Colgate.
"A very pretty story with some pathetic scenes in it."—SATURDAY REVIEW.

THE FAMILY COACH

With Four Full-page Illustrations by J. F. WEEDON. Bevelled
boards, cloth gilt, price 3s.

3/-

A story of a family of children, their schemes and plans, and the
misfortunes that consequently ensue, in the course of a journey from
London to Mentone, where they are to meet their parents, who have just
returned from India.
"'The Family Coach' is as attractive within as without."—TIMES.

GOLDHANGER WOODS

A Child's Romance. With Two Full-page Illustrations.
Bevelled boards, cloth gilt, price 2s.

2/-

"Goldhanger Woods" is the story of the romantic adventure of a
young girl a hundred years ago among a band of desperate smugglers.
"This 'child's romance' is ingeniously planned and well executed."—SPECTATOR.

MRS. DIMSDALE'S GRANDCHILDREN

With Four Full-page Illustrations by C. J. STANILAND.
Bevelled boards, cloth gilt, price 3s.

3/-

A large number of Mrs. Dimsdale's grandchildren are gathered
together one Christmas at the Downs House in Sussex. Milly, in emula-
tion of Aunt Hetty, writes a play. Difficulties intervene, but everything
comes right in the end, and the story concludes with an account of the
acting.
"Full of stir and spirit."—GUARDIAN.

NATIONAL SOCIETY'S DEPOSITORY, SANCTUARY, WESTMINSTER.

BY M. BRAMSTON

Author of "A Woman of Business," "Rosamond Ferrars," &c.

THE STORY OF A CAT AND A CAKE

2/6

With Three Full-page Illustrations by W. S. STACEY. Bevelled boards, cloth gilt, price 2s. 6d.

A story of Nuremberg in the time of the Thirty Years' War, containing adventures and perils in plenty and giving some effective pictures of city and country life in Germany a couple of centuries ago.

"This is a story of the siege of Nuremberg, told with the skill which Miss Bramston always shows in her presentations of life whether past or present."—SPECTATOR.

THEIR FATHER'S WRONG

2/6

With Three Full-page Illustrations by C. J. STANILAND. Bevelled boards, cloth gilt, price 2s. 6d.

The story of the children of a man who had been gradually entangled in a dynamite conspiracy, and of their successful endeavour to repair, as far as possible, the wrong and suffering which their father's action had brought upon innocent people.

"We like this story better than anything that the author has yet given us."
EDUCATIONAL TIMES.

WINNING HIS FREEDOM

2/6

With Three Full-page Illustrations by W. S. STACEY. Bevelled boards, cloth gilt, price 2s. 6d.

The lesson taught by Miss Bramston's story is that of honesty and truth at all costs, as shown in the way in which young Piers Aylward freed himself, after much pain and trouble, from the slavery imposed upon him by his cowardly cousin Henderson.

"'Winning his Freedom' is an admirable book for schoolboys."—RECORD.

LOTTIE LEVISON

2/-

With Two Full-page Illustrations by W. S. STACEY. Bevelled boards, cloth gilt, price 2s.

A South London story for young women and elder girls, describing how Lottie Levison was filled with a longing to teach others the means of getting the happiness which she had gained for herself.

"An excellent story with a fine and unhackneyed moral. . . . Lottie is a very real and very inspiring heroine."—MONTHLY PACKET.

THE ADVENTURES OF DENIS

2/6

With Three Full-page Illustrations by J. F. WEEDON. Bevelled boards, cloth gilt, price 2s. 6d.

The adventures in question are closely connected with the rising of 1745 and the retreat of Prince Charles Edward from Derby to the north again.

"'The Adventures of Denis' is a charming tale of 1745, which would delight any one to read."—SATURDAY REVIEW.

NATIONAL SOCIETY'S DEPOSITORY, SANCTUARY, WESTMINSTER

BY M. BRAMSTON—*continued*

ABBY'S DISCOVERIES

With Three Full-page Illustrations by W. S. STACEY. Bevelled
boards, cloth gilt, price 2s. 6d.

2/6

The story of the successive discoveries, in very ordinary matters, that
little Abigail made in her earliest years, and the meaning and lessons
which they have for all those concerned in bringing up the young.

"We have not seen a better book about the feelings and experiences of childhood
than this since we read the 'My Childhood' of Madame Michelet."—SPECTATOR.

A VILLAGE GENIUS

A True Story of Oberammergau. With Two Full-page Illustrations by J. F. WEEDON. Bevelled boards, cloth gilt,
price 2s.

2/-

A tale of Oberammergau and of the life of Rochus Dedler, the com-
poser of the music that is still used at the Passion Play there.

"A sympathetic and charming sketch."—BOOKSELLER.

DANGEROUS JEWELS

With Four Full-page Illustrations by J. F. WEEDON. Bevelled
boards, cloth gilt, price 3s.

3/-

The opening scenes of this story are laid in Brittany at the time of the
great French Revolution, but the scene changes, and the later chapters
give some vivid descriptions of rough life in a lonely hut on the moorlands
of Devonshire.

"Plenty of stirring incident, and the scenes are novel and unhackneyed."
MANCHESTER GUARDIAN.

A PAIR OF COUSINS

With Three Full-page Illustrations by C. J. STANILAND.
Bevelled boards, cloth gilt, price 2s. 6d.

2/6

The pair of cousins are Flower Callaway, who has a weakness for
appearing interesting and attractive in the eyes of others, and Avis
Goldenlea, a healthy-minded girl of real sterling worth.

"The simplicity of Miss Bramston's new story is one of its greatest charms."
SCHOOLMISTRESS.

THE HEROINE OF A BASKET VAN

With Three Full-page Illustrations. Bevelled boards, cloth gilt,
price 2s. 6d.

2/6

The heroine is little Phenie, whom her father, Jonathan Redmoor,
takes with him to travel about the country in his basket van.

"There are plenty of incidents in the tale to interest the reader, and, as such a story
should end, Phenie finds her right place after all."—SCHOOLMASTER.

UNCLE IVAN

With Three Full-page Illustrations. Bevelled boards, cloth
gilt, price 2s. 6d.

2/6

"Uncle Ivan" gives a striking and eventful picture of life in England
and Russia about forty years ago; together with some insight into the
methods of the Russian Government for dealing with political crime.

"A charming book, and one that must give pleasure to boys and girls, not to mention
any of their elders who may take it up to pass an idle hour."—SATURDAY REVIEW.

NATIONAL SOCIETY'S DEPOSITORY, SANCTUARY, WESTMINSTER.

BY M. BRAMSTON—*continued*

SILVER STAR VALLEY

With Four Full-page Illustrations by C. J. Staniland.
3/- Bevelled boards, cloth gilt, price 3*s.*

In this story Miss Bramston gives a striking and vivid picture of life among a mining community in the Rocky Mountains.

"Miss Bramston's story is spirited and interesting throughout."
Saturday Review.

BY C. R. COLERIDGE

Author of "An English Squire," "The Girls of Flaxley," &c.

A BAG OF FARTHINGS

With Two Full-page Illustrations by W. S. Stacey. Bevelled
2/- boards, cloth gilt, price 2*s.*

The "bag of farthings" contains the prizes for which certain boys and girls run races, and some of the coins become mingled and interchanged with three gold napoleons that are lost. The story tells how Bertie Brown is wrongfully suspected of theft, and how at length he discovers the real culprit and clears his own character.

"The delicate touch with which these pictures are handled is worthy of all praise.'
Spectator.

MAX, FRITZ, AND HOB

With Four Full-page Illustrations by W. S. Stacey. Bevelled
3/- boards, cloth gilt, price 3*s.*

A tale of adventure four hundred years ago, the scene of which is laid principally at the Castle of Lindenberg, in the Bavarian highlands.

"Sure of a welcome from boys. . . . History and fiction are happily blended. . . . The narrative is bright and attractive."—St. James's Gazette.

FIFTY POUNDS

A Sequel to "The Green Girls of Greythorpe." With Four
Full-page Illustrations by W. S. Stacey. Bevelled
3/- boards, cloth gilt, price 3*s.*

A sequel to "The Green Girls of Greythorpe," showing what became of the principal characters in that story after they had grown into young men and young women. The interest of the present story, however, to the reader is in no sense dependent on its predecessor.

"The book is very bright, the story never flags."
Girls' Friendly Society Associates' Journal.

THE GREEN GIRLS OF GREYTHORPE

With Four Full-page Illustrations by C. J. Staniland.
3/- Bevelled boards, cloth gilt, price 3*s.*

A story of an old endowed institution that has come under the notice of the Charity Commissioners, who decide that a reorganisation and extension of the school is necessary, and that the education it affords must be brought into harmony with modern requirements.

"The story is very prettily told, and, although quiet in tone, contains a full share of incident and interest."—Standard.

NATIONAL SOCIETY'S DEPOSITORY, SANCTUARY, WESTMINSTER.

BY C. R. COLERIDGE—*continued*

MAUD FLORENCE NELLIE

Or, Don't Care. With Four Full-page Illustrations by C. J. STANILAND. Bevelled boards, cloth gilt, price 3*s*. **3/-**

A story, showing how a veritable scapegrace of a boy, Harry Whittaker, and his careless sister, Florrie, are gradually brought to see the costs that may be entailed by the spirit which says " Don't care" to every gentle correction of a fault.

REUBEN EVERETT

With Four Full-page Illustrations by C. J. STANILAND. Bevelled boards, cloth gilt, price 2*s*. 6*d*. **2/6**

Miss Coleridge's " Reuben Everett" is the story of " a truant bird, that thought his home a cage," and describes the early days of training colleges and railways in England.

"'Reuben Everett' is a story remarkably true to life."—RECORD.

BY MARY H. DEBENHAM

Author of " The Princesses of Penruth," &c.

TWO MAIDEN AUNTS

With Two Full-page Illustrations by GERTRUDE D. HAMMOND. Bevelled boards, cloth gilt, price 2*s*. **2/-**

The " Maiden Aunts" are two girls, Angelica and Betty Wyndham, upon whom (owing to a series of misfortunes) devolves the bringing up of little Godfrey, the only child of their brother.

"A charming story. . . . All the characters in the book are well delineated. . . . Miss Debenham may well be congratulated."—ST. JAMES'S GAZETTE.

THE MAVIS AND THE MERLIN

With Two Full-page Illustrations by W. S. STACEY. Bevelled boards, cloth gilt, price 2*s*. **2/-**

In "'The Mavis and the Merlin" Miss Debenham gives some graphic pictures of the storm that raged in the Low Countries during the latter half of the sixteenth century, when William the Silent was making his resolute attempt to found the Dutch Republic.

"A spirited tale of the Dutch struggle for liberty under William of Orange. . . . The climax . . . is well worked up and most exciting."—MANCHESTER GUARDIAN.

MY GOD-DAUGHTER

With Two Full-page Illustrations by W. S. STACEY. Bevelled boards, cloth gilt, price 2*s*. **2/-**

" My God-daughter" is little Theodosia (the motherless child of some strolling players) named after the god-mother, Miss Theodosia Cartaret. The story relates how the players' children were lost and found again, in London, at the time when the Gordon Riots were at their height.

"Miss Debenham has a very graceful way of telling her stories. . . . This is a most attractive little book."—JOURNAL OF EDUCATION.

NATIONAL SOCIETY'S DEPOSITORY, SANCTUARY, WESTMINSTER.

Two Maiden Aunts

BY MARY H. DEBENHAM—*continued*

MOOR AND MOSS

With Three Full-page Illustrations by W. S. STACEY. Bevelled boards, cloth gilt, price 2s. 6d.

2/6

A story of the Border in the first half of the sixteenth century, of the struggles that were for ever taking place there and the raids that were being made.

"A story of high courage and reckless daring. . . . For its historical interest and literary charm, a book to be heartily commended."—WESTERN ANTIQUARY.

FOR KING AND HOME

With Three Full-page Illustrations by J. F. WEEDON. Bevelled boards, cloth gilt, price 2s. 6d.

2/6

Of the rising in La Vendée during the great French Revolution, and of the adventures that subsequently befell a well-to-do family there, together with an English cousin Dorothy, who was staying at the château at the time.

"The events are well combined and cleverly conceived."—MANCHESTER GUARDIAN.

MISTRESS PHIL

With Two Full-page Illustrations by C. O. MURRAY. Bevelled boards, cloth gilt, price 2s.

2/-

"Mistress Phil" is Phillis Juliana Cheviot, and the story describes her stay at Waltham Cross in the year 1760, and the results that followed from it, giving also some lively pictures of mail-coaches and highwaymen.

"A book good enough for anybody to read, of whatever age."
SCHOOL BOARD CHRONICLE.

A LITTLE CANDLE

With Five Full-page Illustrations by W. S. STACEY. Bevelled boards, cloth gilt, price 3s. 6d.

3/6

Miss Debenham's story is concerned with Scotland in the stormy days of Claverhouse. The "Little Candle" is Bride Galbraith, who, by her tenderness and grace, softens the time of trial and affliction.

"The character (of Bride Galbraith) is a very beautiful one, and Miss Debenham has drawn it with exquisite touch."—PUBLISHERS' CIRCULAR.

FAIRMEADOWS FARM

With Two Full-page Illustrations by W. S. STACEY. Bevelled boards, cloth gilt, price 2s.

2/-

The scene is laid in Hampshire about the time of Monmouth's rebellion. The story gives some vivid pictures of the opening at Winchester of Judge Jeffreys' harsh campaign against the rebels, and of the clouds that hung over the neighbourhood for a time in consequence.

"A simple yet capitally related story, and the pathetic features are very effectively realised."—LIVERPOOL COURIER.

ST. HELEN'S WELL

With Two Full-page Illustrations by C. J. STANILAND. Bevelled boards, cloth gilt, price 2s.

2/-

"St. Helen's Well" is a story of events that followed the rising in 1745 in favour of the Young Pretender.

"The perils and hardships of the adventure are graphically described."—GUARDIAN.

NATIONAL SOCIETY'S DEPOSITORY, SANCTUARY, WESTMINSTER.

BY FREDERICK C. BADRICK

Author of "Starwood Hall," "The Spanish Galleon," &c.

THE PUFF OF WIND

With Two Full-page Illustrations by C. J. STANILAND.
Bevelled boards, cloth gilt, price 1s. 6d.

1/6

A tale of harbour and heath in the west country a hundred years ago, telling of the evil treatment of Oliver Mackworth and of the strange happening by means of which justice was meted out to the guilty.

"The writing shows a strong sense of 'style' and a quaintness which touches originality."—SATURDAY REVIEW.

THE GOLDEN BUCKLE

With Five Full-page Illustrations by W. S. STACEY. Bevelled boards, cloth gilt, price 3s. 6d.

3/6

A story of London in the year of the Great Plague, showing how one John Garside, a hosier in Holborn, and his family took refuge on board *The Golden Buckle*, then lying on the river.

"All who recollect the dramatic power of the author's 'Peckover's Mill' will heartily greet 'The Golden Buckle,' telling of London in the year of the Great Plague, and the life of the shop-keeping class in the latter half of the seventeenth century."

LEEDS MERCURY.

KING'S FERRY

In the Days of the Press-gang. With Three Full-page Illustrations by W. S. STACEY. Bevelled boards, cloth gilt, price 2s. 6d.

2/6

Concerning a certain ship's doctor who came to Weymouth in press-gang days, and, staying at King's Ferry, tempted Simon Lydgate, the ferryman, to do wrong; of the punishment that fell on Lydgate, and of the joy and peace that followed the home-coming of his boy, Wat.

"Like its predecessors, this volume is full of picturesque pictures of old life and manners."—TIMES.

JOAN'S VICTORY

With Two Full-page Illustrations by J. F. WEEDON. Bevelled boards, cloth gilt, price 1s. 6d.

1/6

Descriptive of a young woman of quick, passionate temper and stubborn purpose, and of the means by which a young child unconsciously brought her back to her better self and helped to soften her heart.

"Admirably detailed. Joan is really a very powerful psychological study."

SPECTATOR.

PECKOVER'S MILL

A Story of the Great Frost of 1739. With Five Full-page Illustrations by W. S. STACEY. Bevelled boards, cloth gilt, price 3s. 6d.

3/6

A story of a Jacobite conspiracy that was on foot in the time of the great frost of 1739, showing how Silas Peckover came home from abroad and took possession of the home of his forefathers, and how the sweet womanliness and honesty of Mistress Ruth influenced him for good.

"Silas Peckover is a character quite worthy of Ainsworth."—ACADEMY.

NATIONAL SOCIETY'S DEPOSITORY, SANCTUARY, WESTMINSTER.

BY FREDERICK C. BADRICK—*continued*

CHRIS DERRICK

2/-
A Stormy Passage in a Boy's Life. With Two Full-page Illustrations by W. S. STACEY. Bevelled boards, cloth gilt, price 2s.

This story supplies some lively sketches of what a mutiny often led to at the beginning of the present century, and of the narrow shifts that smugglers ran in escaping from the revenue officers.

"A spirited story of adventure."—SPECTATOR.

STARWOOD HALL

2/-
A Boy's Adventure. With Two Full-page Illustrations by C. J. STANILAND. Bevelled boards, cloth gilt, price 2s.

A stirring story of how an honest boy fell into the clutches of a band of highwaymen, or "gentlemen of fortune," in the middle of the last century.

"The pictures of rural manners . . . strike us as being extremely life-like."—TIMES.

BY ESMÈ STUART

Author of "The Little Brown Girl," "The Belfry of St. Jude's," &c.

A SMALL LEGACY

2/-
With Two Full-page Illustrations by J. F. WEEDON. Bevelled boards, cloth gilt, price 2s.

A story for children, describing the life led by the coastguardsmen and their families at St. Alban's Head, and showing how it is possible for boys and girls to be brave and honourable in all their actions.

"The picture of the quaint little American is most skilfully drawn, and his quaint sayings are throughout very amusing."—EDUCATIONAL TIMES.

A NEST OF ROYALISTS

1/6
With Two Full-page Illustrations by J. F. WEEDON. Cloth boards, gilt, price 1s. 6d.

A story of Blois in the year 1832, of an English family—the Merediths —who went to live there, and of the circumstances under which they became connected with a Royalist plot against the rule of Louis Philippe.

"A story of historical interest, going back to 1832 or thereabouts. . . . An amusing and instructive volume for the young folks."—WESTERN ANTIQUARY.

THE SILVER MINE

3/-
An Underground Story. With Four Full-page Illustrations by W. S. STACEY. Bevelled boards, cloth gilt, price 3s.

An account of life on the rocky Devonshire coast, an unsuccessful attempt to reopen a disused silver mine, and a long-standing family feud between the Redwoods and the Pennants, with the incidents that served to bring it to an end.

"A very bright, attractive story. The children are natural, and the style is fresh and spirited."—JOURNAL OF EDUCATION.

NATIONAL SOCIETY'S DEPOSITORY, SANCTUARY, WESTMINSTER.

16 NATIONAL SOCIETY'S NEW STORY BOOKS FOR THE YOUNG

BY M. E. PALGRAVE—*continued*

A PROMISE KEPT

With Four Full-page Illustrations. Bevelled boards, cloth gilt,
price 2s. 6d.

2/6

A story with a lofty purpose, showing the amount of self-denial that
is necessary in those who leave their home and kindred to engage in
missionary work in far-off lands.

"Its tone is elevated and serious. Its purpose is to show the need of aiming at
a high standard of life, and the failure of those who only dream noble things."
NATIONAL CHURCH.

BY PENELOPE LESLIE

Author of "Marjory's White Rat," &c.

DOROTHY'S STEPMOTHER

With Frontispiece by C. J. STANILAND. Cloth boards, gilt,
price 1s.

1/-

Motherless little Dorothy went into the wood to look for fairies, and
found instead a very amiable young lady who eventually filled up the
vacant place in the home and brought sunshine into Dorothy's life again.

"This is a simple and pleasant little story of how a little girl cherishes great hopes
and finds them fulfilled in a quite unexpected way."—SPECTATOR.

TROUBLESOME COUSINS

With Frontispiece by W. S. STACEY. Cloth boards, gilt, price 1s.

1/-

"Troublesome Cousins" is a story specially suited for very young
children, and describes some of the scrapes in which Stella Weston and
her cousin Guy found themselves, partly through their restlessness and
partly through their desire to be independent.

"The various incidents are amusing, and the interest of the reader is well main-
tained. . . . A very acceptable gift-book with a good moral tendency."
SCHOOLMASTER.

THE ARTIST OF CROOKED ALLEY

By AUDREY CURTIS, Author of "Little Miss Curlylocks."
With Two Full-page Illustrations by GERTRUDE D.
HAMMOND. Cloth boards, gilt, price 1s. 6d.

1/6

The artist was only nine years old and lived in Crooked Alley; his
canvas was the pavement of a London street, his colours no more than a
motley collection of odds and ends of coloured chalks.

"A story of exceptional interest: one that attracts and retains the reader from
beginning to end."—TEACHERS' AID.

LOST ON THE MOOR

1/-

By "TAFFY." With Frontispiece. Cloth boards, gilt, price 1s.
The story of Little Jack, how he was lost on the moor in a thick fog
through his brother's disobedience, and how he was found and finally
restored to his home.

"An evening will be very pleasantly spent and attended with much good in reading
this interesting story."—SCHOOLMASTER.

NATIONAL SOCIETY'S DEPOSITORY, SANCTUARY, WESTMINSTER.